HERO'S TALE

BLOOD

&

THUNDER

R.J. Knight

All heroes are deserving of a tale. And every tale of a hero. But alas, so many tales have no true hero, and so many heroes never receive a tale. This is a great tragedy. The lives and deaths of heroes ought to be told boldly and often. For from them men and women draw strength and inspiration. We are encouraged to be better versions of ourselves.

Sad is the kingdom that forgets those rare few of uncommon courage who came from them. Sad is the person who believes heroes are born. Such forgetfulness is a great crime, and such thinking a lie. Heroes are not born. They are made. And not from fine ore or precious substance either. No. Heroes are made from the same flesh and bone as you and I. Blood and sweat. Tears and heartbreak. Emotion, weakness, failures, thoughts, hopes, dreams, defeats, and experiences. All of these forge a hero, just as they forge us.

So let me tell you a story of a hero who has suffered many such pains and heartaches. Who has watched what he loves torn away from him, and knows full well the taste of defeat.

This is the beginning of the tale of Jadu; a tale of blood… and thunder.

Contents

The Origin of Jadu
- a tale of Jadu, the Mighty Hound

The cry that broke the sky that day was something that would engrave itself into legend. Powerful, feral, heart-wrenching. It was a cry filled with all bitter emotions. A scream of pain and regret. A shout of agony and inner death. It was a cry from a dying heart – the death throes of happiness within a single, unfortunate soul.

It was the cry of the Pak that would one day be known as the Mighty Hound, Jadu. But that day he was no legend, and he was no hero. That day he held the dead body of his father in his own trembling hands, and let out the cry that marked the beginning of his tale…

The morning that would eventually lead to that moment was just as any other. He was awoken by his father before the dawn, and the two of them went out into the woods to begin their daily ritual of sparring.

The early air was crisp and unusually cool, with a thin mist hanging in the branches. As Jadu's father handed him the stout fir rod that he would be using to spar, the younger Pak's stomach growled, and he wished he could be somewhere warmer and with more food.

Jadu and his father were both of the Pak race of demi-humans, natives of their species' homeland, Tarfa. The Pak stand with the same stature as a human, only they have the head, legs, tale, claws, and fur of a dog. Despite these bestial traits, they are no less intelligent or graceful, and no more savage than most other races of Alataran.

Jadu's father was the Alpha Male of their pack, and was a beloved one at that, both for his physical strength and his excellent leadership. He stood a full head and shoulders taller than most men and was built like a mountain of muscle and sinew. His nose was short as well as his ears, and his fur was black.

4

Jadu had inherited some of his father's size and bulk, but was still far smaller than the burly Alpha, even though he was larger than most. His fur was dark brown, with a red-tan patch over his right eye, another on his right hip, and a third covering his entire left foot. His nose was longer than his fathers, and his ears droopier.

That morning, as afore mentioned, was like any other. The two sparred one another in the cool mist of the woodland dawn, each armed with a wooden rod that they wielded as though it were a sword. The strikes were painful because they wore neither armor nor heavy clothing – only trousers and tunics – and the mist was additionally chilling for the same reason, soaking through their warm fur and clinging to their flesh after the first half hour.

In the midst of the fight, Jadu deflected a strike and attacked in retribution, only to find his leg slapped painfully with his father's weapon and his own blow parried. The younger Pak leapt back and huffed in exertion.

"Jadu, at least try." His father said in a deep, resounding voice.

"I am trying." Jadu replied.

"Not with your full attention you are not. You are fighting with only half your heart."

Jadu groaned.

"What do you want?" He demanded, an old irritation suddenly breaking loose. "I am a good warrior, at least as good as the soldiers. I can fight, I can lead, I know math, and the merchants, and how to identify good trades from bad, how to hunt, how to track – by my ears I can even read and write! What is the purpose of this daily training? I get no better."

Jadu's father sighed deeply.

"Son," He began. "our time in this world is short. With strength we may live to sixty years, with providence to eighty. But fortune is so fickle, and most do not live past forty years. We never know when we may cease from the earth, to be gone, never to return. And when that time comes for me, I want to know I am leaving this pack to someone I trust. I trust no one more than you, son."

This time Jadu was the one to sigh.

"I know father, you have told me so before." He answered quietly. "But what more do I have to accomplish before you consider me ready? How am I still in need of training? I am a grown man! Twenty years of age. In what way am I lacking?"

The Alpha's reply was stunning.

"It is because you think you are ready, that you are not."

Jadu's mouth hung open slightly. *What?* He wondered. *But if I am ready, then what else am I supposed to think?*

"Father, that makes no sense." He said.

The tiniest smile flicked across the bigger Pak's austere face, but then quickly vanished.

"Jadu, do you remember when you thought you were able to defeat me?"

Jadu thought back to that moment. He remembered it well. Three years ago. He had come back to his home from a sparring match and ravenously tore into a piece of smoked fowl. His mother, a thin, tan Pak with a pointy nose had walked into the room as well a moment later.

"How was todays sparring?" She had asked.

Jadu swallowed and then replied "Good, but I think it's pointless."

"Oh, and why is that?"

"Because I could win."

Jadu was uncertain, but he could have sworn his mother chuckled when he said that.

"Are you so sure?" She asked in a sweet, honeylike voice that he was accustomed to, but with a hidden undertone of amusement.

Jadu nodded.

"Without doubt." He said. "Therefore, it is of no point for him to keep taking me out there every morning. If it were an actual fight, I could beat him. I hardly ever receive blows any more in our spars even. It's just such a waste of time."

"Love, your father is trying to teach you to be a great warrior. You never know when-"

"When I'll need to protect my family, myself, or my pack." Jadu interrupted. "I know, I know."

His mother frowned and, just then, his father entered.

"Good match today Jadu." The big Pak said sincerely but without a smile. "You're starting to become quite the fighter."

Jadu rolled his eyes and said nothing. When there was no spoken response, his father stopped and looked back and forth between him and his mother. Finally, the Alpha Male crossed his arms and asked: "What is it?"

"Jadu feels these daily sparring matches are pointless." Jadu's mother told her mate.

"Oh?" The young Pak's father asked, turning to face him. "Why?"

Jadu swallowed another piece of meat.

"Because I can win too easily."

His father's eyes narrowed.

"You think you're a better fighter than me already?" He asked humorlessly.

Jadu had nodded.

Coming back from the memory, standing across from his father three years after that incident with a bruise forming on his leg, he could still remember the broken bones that had ensued in their "real spar" and wondered how he had been so stupid as to think his father had actually been showing his true strength before that point.

"I was an idiot then." Jadu admitted.

His father smiled faintly before becoming impassive again.

"But at the moment you believed you were ready. However, when tested, you found you were still lacking. Do you understand now?"

Jadu thought it over for a few moments and then shook his head.

"I will never be a better warrior than you. I understand that now. Are you trying to say I will never be as good an Alpha either?"

Jadu's father groaned in frustration and turned around as though to leave.

"No, Jadu," He said. "I am trying to say that you should always give everything your absolute best. Always be trying to improve yourself."

"What does that have to do with being ready?"

Before Jadu's father could respond, a sudden howl cut through the still morning. As Pak, Jadu and his father could feel the intent behind the howl; even so far as to recognized if it was benign or malignant to themselves. And this howl was no doubt of the second kind. It was a dark howl. A savage howl. A hungry, ferocious, primitive howl. A howl that sounded like death.

Jadu and his father looked at each other with eyes wide. A second howl, like the first but from a different source, rang out from the same direction. A third and fourth soon followed, then many more. The two Pak shared an unspoken agreement through their eyes, then turned and sprinted toward the sound, weaving through the woodland with deft skill.

Seconds passed in a blur and the two emerged at their village.

The village, which consisted of a good twenty dwellings and a few businesses, was in an uproar. Wooden houses were ablaze and smoking, and the villagers were in a frenzy to flee. The source of it all was clear. Eight Pak, all of them with jet black fur, armed with swords, and wearing crude iron armor with yellow sashes, were ravaging it with torch and blade.

Only four village guards were ever on watch at one time, and two of them could already be seen lying dead when Jadu and his father arrived. The remaining defenders were easily identified by their white uniforms, and were doing battle with the invaders, their halberds providing a strong advantage against their adversary's comparatively short swords.

After only the briefest of pauses to take all of this in, Jadu's father let out a howl of his own. Unlike the howls from before, which were from the black Pak, this howl was benign to Jadu. His father's howl was powerful beyond compare, unmatched by any other Pak he had ever met; to his enemies it spelled certain defeat, but to his allies… the strength it filled their hearts with was incredible.

With this strength inside him Jadu felt inspired, encouraged, fearless! Riding this wave of might he released his own howl – strong, but nothing compared to his father's. Within moments he heard more joining him, every man, woman, and child of their village taking up the mantle alongside their Alpha and his son. The legion of howls was like a chorus of power and unity. Each member of the pack felt the courage and vitality of the others well up inside of them!

Jadu finished his howl before many of the others and, looking down he saw that his father had already rushed into the fray, pouncing upon one of the invaders. With his fellows still howling around him, Jadu followed his sire's footsteps, dashing recklessly towards the battle.

However, before he reached the melee, he noticed one of the attackers, separate from the others, assailing a young maiden, and ran towards him with all speed. Jadu's enemy spotted his approach and turned, swinging his blade. Jadu ducked beneath the strike and slashed up at his opponent's face with his claws. He felt his strong nails connect with flesh and pull through. Certainly not lethal, but enough to distract.

His swing complete, Jadu leapt back, narrowly evading a retributory strike from the black Pak's sword. By that time, the maiden had successfully fled, leaving only Jadu and his foe.

The injured invader felt his bleeding face with his spare hand and then growled at Jadu angrily. Jadu growled back. The wounded warrior then lifted his sword as though to lunge and strike, but was stopped short as a halberd ended his life.

Jadu took a deep breath, and turned to see a young Pak about his age standing a short distance from him. The white uniform shirt with a somewhat high collar marked him as one of the guards. But to Jadu, he was more than that. The white and brown spotted dog in front of him with a stupid grin on his face was Hanny, the village jokester.

In Pak culture, all of the children are raised together, regardless of the station or rank of their parents. This leads to strong bonds formed between cohorts, to the point where most Pak consider these fellows of theirs' brothers and sisters even into adulthood. Being nearly the same age, Jadu and Hanny were two such Pak – brothers by nurture and not nature.

"I saw you saving my cousin and decided to help." Hanny said with a smooth, casual tone, leaning on his weapon like a staff. "Are you finally trying to get a mate? There are better ways to impress women."

Jadu rolled his eyes.

"Now is not the time for humor, Hanny."

The white dog sighed as though in disappointment.

"Yeah, you're right."

The guard took back up his weapon and looked down towards the fallen Pak. Jadu followed his gaze.

"You ever killed anyone before?" Hanny asked.

Jadu shook his head grimly. "I am glad it was you, not me." He said.

"Well, let's hope it stays that way."

Without another word the guard turned and ran back towards the thick of the fight. Jadu, for his part, snatched the dead invader's sword from his hands and then followed. But, again, just before he rushed into the battle himself, his ears twitched. He had heard a faint sound. *A scream?* Turning, he saw two new Pak, both black and armored like the others, sneaking into a two-story stone house on the far end of the village, the only stone house in the village, *his* house.

"Mother!"

Without a moment of hesitation, Jadu rushed towards the structure, his legs moving with speed they normally could not muster. He reached the building in only seconds and ran through the wooden door, which had already been broken down. He heard metallic

11

footsteps above him and immediately dashed to the staircase, not pausing to look around the bottom story. He took the steps three or four at a time and reached their top within moments.

The stairs came out into an open room about as wide as eight men shoulder to shoulder in both directions, with one door directly across from them leading to a balcony, and another door to one side that led to the master bedroom. When Jadu arrived, one of the two invaders was standing in the main room at the top of the stairs, and the other was just coming from the bedroom, blood dripping from his sword.

Fear and anger flooded into Jadu's mind, blinding his reason and clouding his judgement. With a savage growl he lunged upon the nearest of his adversaries, hacking and slashing wildly, with total disregard for method, morality, and his own limited energy. The defending Pak had been prepared for his assault, but not for the power and emotion behind it. His blade was batted out of the way whenever he tried to lift it, and after only a few seconds he lay dead on the ground, his armor beaten in at places and his unguarded head mauled as though by an animal.

Jadu turned from this vicious frenzy just in time to see the second invader slashing at him. He blocked the attack and then countered. The swing dented the armor on his opponent's shoulder but left him vulnerable for a split second too long, allowing his foe to slash him across the chest.

Jadu howled in pain and pulled back. The injury was not severe or very deep, but it was long and hurt badly.

The young Pak growled at his opponent, who was smiling sadistically, as though relishing his pain. With a cry of anger Jadu lunged again, slashing with all his strength. The armored Pak deftly evaded, and would have ended Jadu's life that very moment had he not stumbled over a wicker basket upon the floor.

Seizing the tiny opportunity, Jadu swung twice at his foe and then thrust. The first two slashes were parried, but the thrust struck true and plunged straight into the black Pak's heart. The invader fell lifelessly to the ground and Jadu, leaving his sword in the corpse rather than taking the time to pull it out, ran into the bedroom.

His fears were true, and he dropped to his knees as the nightmare before him swallowed all of his will and half of his heart in a single bite.

His mother lay dead on the floor.

Several seconds of oblivion passed. Then… Jadu crawled forward slowly on his hands and knees, whimpering. He approached his mother's still body and nudged her shoulder with his nose. There was no response. He whimpered again, this time louder, and then nudged her again. Again, nothing. He growled, but to no avail. He even barked at her still features, but she did not turn. Finally, he fell back onto his haunches, covered his eyes, and began to weep.

He had not long mourned when armored footsteps approached him from behind. One of the black Pak stood over him, his breastplate stained with blood. The invader looked down at Jadu, then lifted his sword. Jadu did not care.

There was a cracking sound and then a metallic thud as the black Pak's body fell lifelessly to the ground. Suddenly, Jadu felt a strong hand on his shoulder, and someone hoisted him to his feet.

"Be strong!" A voice hissed in his ear.

Wiping away his tears Jadu turned. Standing beside him was the leader of their pack's military, Red Maw, as he was normally called. He was the second tallest Pak in the pack, second only to Jadu's father. His fur was thin and lightly colored, with a reddish patch across his long snout – thus his nickname. His ears were pointed and his eyes keen. He was a fearsome warrior, perhaps the best.

"Jadu…" Red Maw's voice dropped to a sad whisper as he looked towards the still woman. "I am sorry. Truly." The warrior's voice rose again. "But now is not the time to mourn. I need your strength. Come."

Jadu wiped the tears from his eyes again and followed the older Pak out of the house, both of them moving at a jog. Once outside, Red Maw immediately turned and headed into the forest, Jadu still following close behind. Even as distant as Jadu's mind was at that moment, he could tell clearly that many other Pak had recently been across the ground they were then crossing. He could smell both familiar friends as well as the musk of the black invaders, all of it intermixed with the scent of pain and blood.

The sound of clumsy footsteps crashing through the brush towards him and Red Maw brought Jadu out of his dismal reverie and back into reality. Hanny was stumbling quickly towards them, an arrow in his calf.

"All-King be praised am I glad to see you!" The white dog exclaimed.

Normally Jadu would have rushed forward to help his friend, but at that moment he felt too drained to do even that. However, that weakness would soon fade; a fire had begun to ignite within his belly and was slowly growing. The fire of vengeance.

"Soldier Hanny," Red Maw hailed the guard urgently. "how fairs the battle?"

"Not well I'm afraid." Hanny answered. "We've driven them back to the creek, but they're holding there. Stubborn snags. Alpha took Bondo, Jons, Keekee, Amirah, and Trodo to try to route them or else get them to flee, but it's a close fight."

"Fear not, the Blackhounds will fall." Red Maw replied. "You have done well."

Hanny nodded and then limped over to Jadu.

"You'll need this more than I do." He said, handing him his halberd.

Jadu quietly accepted the weapon with a grateful nod of his head. Hanny, in turn, smiled and then headed back towards the village.

When the young warrior turned around, Red Maw was already waiting. Jadu looked to his superior as though to say "I'm ready", and the two continued on their way, now running, the sound of battle audible in the distance.

"You called them Blackhounds?" Jadu asked as they ran.

"Aye. They are a savage pack from the south, brutal and vicious. How they got to us, I do not know. The Amboros and Chila Packs should have blocked them at the least."

Jadu snorted angrily. The fire within him was by that time raging, and he found himself impatient to feel Blackhound blood on his hands and its smell in his nose – a dramatic change from someone who had never killed, and in such a short time too. But such is the way of heartbreak and vengeance.

"No matter, we'll butcher them just the same." He said with a voice like ice.

Red Maw made no reply, and soon the two of them could hear the clang of blades and howls of the injured clearly. A few more seconds and they burst into the clearing where the battle was taking place. It was a long clearing, but fairly narrow; perhaps sixty or seventy paces across in total, with a small stream running through its center.

At least a dozen Pak lay dead across the space, and a few more lay to the side of the battle wounded. The remaining combatants consisted of Jadu's father, three other Pak that Jadu recognized as part of their military, though they were not in uniform, two other members of his pack, and four of the Blackhound soldiers in their crudely forged iron armor.

Red Maw howled and then rushed into the fray. Jadu would have followed for the third time that day, save he noticed a fifth Blackhound standing to the back of the melee, a bow in his hands and a quiver on his back. As he watched, the black dog released an arrow from his bow, which plunged into the side of one of Jadu's companions, slowing him just enough to be finished off by the Blackhound he was fighting.

Jadu growled in fury and spun his halberd in his hand. Taking aim, he threw the great weapon with all his might and skill. Although not designed for such a throw, it flew true, and struck the archer squarely in the chest, the spearhead punching straight through his iron breastplate and bringing him to the ground in a heap. With a howl of victory, Jadu joined the fight, clawing and biting like a mad wolf.

The ensuing frenzy was chaotic and maddening, a whirlwind of carnage and blades. During its course, the young Pak received several slashes across his chest, back, and arms, but none of them severe. At some point he picked up a sword from of one of his fallen foes and began to use it in place of his claws and fangs, though exactly when he could not remember. After only few minutes, however, only one Blackhound remained, and Jadu's father led the remaining soldiers in encircling him.

Glancing around, Jadu noticed that he, his father, Red Maw, and one other of his pack were all that remained. He dared not wonder if the others were dead or only injured, and he feared what names would be on those two lists when the battle was over. Just then, a loud, arrogant, dreadful voice called out. It was not speaking to them though – it was speaking to everything.

Turning, Jadu caught sight of a black Pak wearing a dark red robe and an iron breastplate, standing at the edge of the clearing. In the newcomer's hand was a staff made of bone, with a trio of human and demi-human skulls fastened to the top, along with feathers and scraps of fur. The strange Pak lifted his grisly scepter high and shouted out more unusual words, none of them in a language Jadu knew.

Suddenly, out of the bone-forged staff issued a pulse of red light that swept across the entire clearing. Immediately the bodies of the fallen, both of Jadu's pack and the Blackhounds, started to stir, and then, with a unified groan that was unnatural and altogether horrifying, they began to rise.

The surrounded Blackhound soldier howled as though in triumph and then lunged at the ring of defenders that had encircled him. He managed to slash Jadu's father's wrist with his initial attack, but was quickly cut down by Red Maw. That threat dealt with, the four warriors turned and retreated until they were all back to back, facing the standing corpses that now surrounded them.

"Freakers." Red Maw said grimly. "They are a mindless and violent form of undead. Watch yourselves."

Jadu once more growled angrily, and readied his blade in front of him.

"Everything was so normal this morning." The Pak beside him whimpered. "Why did this all have to happen?"

"Be strong." Jadu's father encouraged him without taking his eyes off of the freakers, who had by then begun to circle them.

During the apparent lull, Jadu took a closer look at one of the creatures. Its eyes were rolled back in its head, its jaw was slack, its movements were sporadic and strange – as though it had no balance – and red-purple light glowed from its mouth. *How dare he defile the bodies of my friends!* The young Pak thought.

"Jadu, with me. We kill their witchdoctor."

Jadu glanced at his father. The older Pak's eyes were locked on the dog in red standing at the other side of the clearing, a dozen undead between them. Even in his state of vengeful rage, Jadu could see the odds before him clearly enough, and knew, that while it was their best chance, the likelihoods of survival were slim. This thought led to another.

"Father…" He began sadly. "I need to tell you something."

Jadu's father must have heard the importance in his son's tone, because he waited for him to finish.

"I tried to stop them but… I could not and… I'm sorry… they killed mother…"

The shout that escaped Jadu's father's mouth at that moment startled him. It was a shout of rage and brokenness, and before he or anyone else could ever even consider to act, the burly Alpha had charged into the mob of freakers before him.

"Father!" Jadu cried as he rushed after him, slashing at the nearest monster.

No longer was he filled with rage or fury, but fear. The thought of losing his father as well crashed upon him like the greatest of waves. Ahead of him, the young Pak could see the massive warrior fighting through the swarm of undead as they assailed him from every side with the weapons they still held. Although the giant of an Alpha cleaved and swung with mighty blows, felling the monsters rapidly, for every foe he brought down, a new injury appeared on his body, more grievous than the last.

"FATHER!" Jadu screamed again, cutting down a freaker after parrying its thrust.

He rushed to reach the Alpha, but two more of the monsters stepped into his path, their mouths hanging open and their tongues rolled out lifelessly. Jadu stopped in his tracks, and then rushed upon them after only a moment of hesitation. He received a slash to his left shoulder, and a thrust pierced through his thigh, but he put down his two foes in a matter of seconds. Looking up, he saw his father's tall frame vanish under a storm of blows, the mighty warrior finally falling beneath the lifeless mob.

"Retreat!" Red Maw ordered from somewhere behind him.

Distantly Jadu could hear the fleeing steps of Red Maw and the remaining soldier, but his mind did not take it in. In fact, his mind did not take in anything. A roar resounded within his skull, along with a howl. Eternal, it seemed, never ending, primal, and powerful. The roar was that of a mighty and fearless creature – an apex predator who would not, who *could* not, be denied. And the howl was the sound of a wolf, somehow different from the pack, strong on its own and mightier than anything else in the woodland around it. Those two sounds, the roar and the howl, echoed in Jadu's empty mind like two shouts in a great cavernous expanse. And then, everything went black for the young warrior.

…

When Jadu awoke some time later, it was with warm sunlight shining across him through the canopy overhead. He opened his eyes, his mind not yet remembering the fighting or the tragedies of hours before. A curious face and gray fur were in front of him. Jadu started in surprise, and immediately they were gone.

Sitting up in the clearing, the young Pak could still smell whoever it was's scent – it was sweet, like flowers. But then a much more repugnant odor struck him, the smell of death.

Remembrance came back to Jadu like a blow from a hammer, and immediately he was on his feet. Looking around he found that he was not in the clearing from before, but rather, a smaller one. However, he could still smell the site of the battle, and it was not far away. Running and limping at once, he made his way as quickly as he could to the battleground, heedless to the fact that he carried no weapon, nor that his wounds had been bandaged and covered with salve.

He reached the clearing where the skirmish had been, and found that the bodies which had been resurrected as freakers, along with the Pak in red, had been torn to pieces as if by some beast. This startled him for but a moment, and then he saw the body of his father. Rushing to the Alpha's side, he fell to his knees and rolled him onto his back.

"Father! Father!" He cried. "Wake up! It is me!"

But as with his mother, the great, burly Pak made no response.

"Father!"

Still it was useless. He was dead.

Jadu's eyes welled up with tears and his heart began to throb. Tilting back his head to face the sky, he released a shout that has become legend. A cry like no other. The woodland beasts and the birds either listened in awe or fled in terror. The village too heard his scream, and indeed, history itself harkened to that bitter wail.

If it is possible for a person to die while their body yet lives, then that was what happened to Jadu in that moment. The power of the bonds between Pak is well known, and respected as some of the strongest in demi-human and humankind. So, if ever you have wondered why some wolves travel alone, wonder no longer. At least for Jadu, it was the pain that drove him from his pack, and towards the adventures that would make him into legend.

He did not return to the village after the battle. He did not wonder what had happened to the Blackhound witchdoctor and his freakers. He did not wonder who it was that had bandaged his wounds and likely saved his life. No. Instead of these things, he hid. He watched the village bury his father and his mother that evening, along with the many others who had died in the raid, each of the graves marked with a wooden cross. With the Alpha dead, Red Maw functioned as the leader over the proceedings, and led the village in their mourning.

Jadu watched as they wept and prayed for the departed, and held his peace as they cried over his own grave, the one that was empty. Although his head drooped some with shame and guilt, he turned his back on the village and left. That village, those people, the local woodland even, and the very air around him had become permeated with the pain of his loss. He could not breathe in the familiar smells, see the familiar sights, or hear the familiar voices without the bodies of his father and his mother reappearing to him in his mind. His heart ached unending, but whene'er he saw them in his mind's eye, it was ripped apart afresh. And so he left – careful to hide his scent and his tracks.

Late that night, back at the village, Red Maw skulked into the woods to meet with a massive Blackhound warrior, easily a half a man taller than Jadu's father had been.

"Satisfied with your betrayal?" The giant asked in a gravelly, booming voice.

"I only wish less of my men needed to be killed in the process." Red Maw replied in frustration. "The deal was for you to kill the Alpha Male and Female. Not slaughter a quarter of the village and kill half of my finest soldiers."

The Blackhound warrior grinned an evil, toothy grin.

"That was your plan, yes." He said.

"My plan?" Red Maw asked, his eyes darting around the dark woodland surrounding him while his hand clutched the hilt of his knife. "This wasn't the deal." He continued, now almost violently, as he turned back to face the giant. "I promised you gold when I was made Alpha."

The titan laughed.

"The Blackhound don't want your gold. We want your land. And we want your blood."

Red Maw's knife was in his hand and held out before him in an instant.

"You can have blood, but it won't be mine." He declared.

The giant laughed again, and as he did so, three more soldiers, none so large, crept out of the woods, surrounding the lone Red Maw with their weapons drawn. The veteran Pak glanced at his adversaries, sizing them up, then turned back to the giant.

"I suggest you listen to our new proposal, pup." The Blackhound growled in cruel malignance.

Meeting Lilula
- a tale of Jadu, the Mighty Hound

Jadu did not sleep at all the night following his parents' death. After watching the funeral processions from his hiding place, he turned his eyes to the south, and set off into the darkness, guided by the stars, the moon, and his natural night vision. Where he was going, he did not know. But he knew he could not remain at that place. Everything about it, everything familiar, was a reminder of those he once loved who were no more.

The injuries from the battle remained with him still. But he did not care. They had been wrapped in a fibrous cloth made from some plant, and covered in an organic salve. Who had done this as he lay unconscious a few hours before was a mystery to him. But he cared not for that either. His mind was elsewhere.

As he trekked into the dark woodland, Jadu's emotions kept him from thinking. For a time he would travel, angry, bitter, and filled with wrath towards the Blackhounds. Then he would become sad and mournful for those he had lost. Then guilt would assail him for not having spent more time with the people who had been taken from him. The next moment he would nearly turn around and head home, longing for the familiar faces. But those familiar faces were gone, and so he pressed on. In the end, however, all of these feelings returned to the first – to vengeance.

And so, enveloped as he was in the many conflicting arguments of his heart, Jadu traveled deeper and deeper into the woods, aware of neither his surroundings nor his wounds, until at last he could bear it no longer, and struck a tree in anger. *Crack-crack-crack-crack…* The midnight forest echoed with the sound of his fist on the strong bark, and that told him: something was wrong.

The overwhelming feel of dread and fear was strong enough to shake him from his reverie of vengeance for the moment. His very instincts screamed at him in alarm, crying out like a night watchman to warn him of danger. Jadu continued to huff in ire, but at the same time he perked up his ears and sniffed the air. His senses warned him of a threat. But what?

Stepping away from the tree with one of his fingers broken by the reckless blow, he looked up towards the clear sky. On the horizon, illuminated by the heavenly bodies overhead, was a giant tree – no more than two miles away.

Now, when I say giant, I mean *giant*. Piercing the clouds and reaching up to the very stars, I, in fact, am referring to nothing other than one of the great Elder Trees. These ancient trees possess vast amounts of unknown power. Beneath their roots, within their trunks, and amongst their branches dwell incredible creatures both spectacular and peculiar. Additionally, the wood, bark, sap, and even leaves of the tree itself are highly sought after by Silvertongues and similar practitioners of the astral arts.

With the enormity of the Elder Trees, one might imagine its resources would be easily claimed. But the truth is not so. You see, the closer one gets to these mighty titans of nature, the more dangerous their road becomes. For those creatures I mentioned previously are not oft friendly to human and demi-human kind.

These things in mind, Jadu saw the giant tree so close, and immediately stepped away from it in reflexive fear, his eyes darting around. He had heard more than one warning of the giant predators that made their nests in the Elder's branches and roots; how with their terrible size and silent movements they could kill a man before he ever had time to scream.

Heh. How foolish. Jadu thought. After all, what were the chances that he would be attacked by such a beast so far from the- There! Blotting out the very light of the moon, a black shadow! But as quickly as it appeared it was gone.

No matter, immediately upon seeing the darting silhouette, Jadu turned and fled away from the Elder Tree. And not a moment too soon. Scarce had he begun to run than mighty talons crashed against the ground where he had been standing, the giant claws missing his tail by but an armslength.

The lone Pak cursed his ill fortune and glanced over his shoulder that he might behold the creature. A giant of an owl, twice his height, with claws large enough to skewer him on one nail, and a beak so powerful and dreadfully sharp he doubted he could survive even a single peck. The monstrous bird shrieked at its fleeing meal, and then flapped its wings and returned to the sky without the slightest further sound.

Turning back to the foliage before him, Jadu ran as quickly as he could through the darkness, harshly scolding himself for being so heedless of his own surroundings.

A few seconds passed in terrible fear, and then: *crack*! Jadu was tackled from the side and brought tumbling to the dirt, just as the terrible owl grasped the air where he had been with its killing talons. Having again missed its prey, the beast withdrew its empty claws, soared by, and vanished into the sky once more. No sooner had it done this, though, than a hand grabbed hold of Jadu's arm and began to tug at him to rise.

"Get up! Get up!" The young woman who had tackled him urged – somehow unafraid. "If you want to live you need to run."

Jadu got back onto his feet quickly and then was pulled along rapidly by the mysterious stranger. After a few seconds she released his hand and sped up. Jadu followed. As near as he could see through the haze of danger, the woman ahead of him was a young Pak maiden, perhaps a few years his junior, with gray fur and dressed in dear skin.

"Do you know how to fight giant owls?" The maiden asked.

"What!" Jadu exclaimed.

"The easy way. Not the hard way, obviously." She replied as though it answered everything. "One of us is bait and the other one jumps on its back, stabs at its heart and-"

"Are you mad!"

"You don't. Ok then, to the right!"

Jadu obeyed the command and dove to his right at the same moment as his companion. The giant owl swerved to avoid the large tree they had just found cover behind and then rejoined the darkness with an angry cry.

"Get up again!"

Jadu lifted himself to his feet to find that the woman had already left him.

"Wait!" He called out.

In a moment he had caught up to her, causing him to realize he was far faster than she. As he pondered this, the maiden glanced at him with – was that a smile? – and then ducked under a fallen log that Jadu instead toppled over, having not noticed it. Catching back up to the other Pak again, Jadu looked quickly around for the owl and then dared to speak.

"Who are you?" He asked.

"Left!"

The woman had not turned to look at him, but instead darted to the side. Jadu panicked and did the same, once more narrowly evading the talons of their hunter.

"My name is Lilula." The maiden offered as she pulled him to his feet and led him along.

Jadu puffed a few deep breaths and then responded. "My name is Jadu."

Beyond that, he was uncertain what to say. Should he thank her? Should he ask what she was doing outside in the middle of the night? Should he inquire where they are going? None of these came out of his mouth because, before he could determine which was best, the Pak known as Lilula began to run faster – indeed, as fast as she could.

"Make it to the cliff." She shouted.

"What?"

Jadu glanced over his shoulder and saw a black silhouette flash before the stars. The dread of facing the giant demon of an owl was enough to silence his uncertainty so that he obeyed the woman beside him without hesitation. Ahead of them he could see a ravine rapidly approaching, and within a moment they were upon it.

"Jump in!"

Jadu began to panic again but, without thinking about it, obeyed and dove over the side of the ravine. Beneath him was open air for many men in height, but, behind him, the owl was swooping in with its talons open and stretched out to grasp hold of its prey. However, that beast would be denied its supper, for the force of nature quickly pulled Jadu down. Down, down, down; plummeting to the base of the canyon while the giant of a bird was blocked by the narrow walls.

Splash! Jadu landed in a deep pool of water and sunk to the bottom. For a few seconds, his mind was frozen. The cool liquid surrounded him, and the fear began to subside. Then he breached the surface, gasping for air, and began to paddle for the land.

Now, while he had plummeted like a stone, the maiden Lilula had descended in a far more graceful manner. A tall, old, dead tree had fallen into the ravine some time ago, forming a steep angle from the bottom all of the way to the top. Over the years the bark had been worn away and the wood weathered smooth. Down this Lilula had slid, the short skirt she was wearing providing an excellent seat. Nearing the bottom, she stopped herself by grabbing hold of one of the old branches, and then swung off onto the ground, her feet touching the soil about the same time Jadu pulled himself out of the water.

Looking up, the soaked dog-man saw that the ravine was only wide enough for four people to walk side by side, and was at least two stories deep, thus stopping the owl from following them because of its incredible wings. Comforted by this, Jadu allowed his head to drop as he remained on his hands and knees panting for some time, water dripping out of his drenched fur.

The maiden Lilula approached him during this reprieve and stopped just short.

"Are you alright?" She asked sincerely.

"I believe so." Jadu answered.

"That's good. I'll start a fire so you can dry off. Just wait there."

Jadu growled faintly to show his displeasure, annoyed some woman he had just met was giving him orders, and then tried to stand. His limbs refused to obey him, greeting him instead with an aching pain all through his entire body.

"Agha-!" The young Pak panted when the soreness hit him.

Near instantly Lilula was beside him and rolling him onto his back. Needless to say, Jadu tried to resist, but his body would not allow him to.

"Dolt." The maiden lectured him. "Your wounds haven't healed and you've been walking despite them all night. The cold water is going to have cramped everything up. You may as well be made of wood right now."

Jadu huffed in pain and then looked towards Lilula with distrust.

"How do you know… about my wounds?" He asked.

The maiden started back.

"I… well… I'm the one who treated them." She replied.

Jadu winced, both in pain and surprise.

"You have been following me since the fight?"

"Well…" Lilula looked away, nervously rubbing her tail. "Just stay there." She finally said, standing up. "I'll go get that firewood."

Jadu opened his maw to speak, but the maiden was already gone. With a sigh he let his head fall onto the rocky ground beneath him and stared up at the sky through the ravine's opening. His mind had been distracted from his anguish of spirit, and he was finally able to think. He had so many questions he had not had only a few minutes before. So, so many questions for the young Pak who had introduced herself as Lilula. Who was she? Why was she following him? Why had she tended his wounds? Why had she saved him from the owl? How did she know the forest so well?

All of these questions were cut down in a single moment as a thought occurred to him: The roar and the howl – the last two sounds he had heard before fainting after the battle – could those have been her?

Impossible. Jadu thought, remembering the state of his enemies when he had awoken and returned to the sight of the skirmish; torn apart, limb from limb.

What manner of beast could do that? He wondered. *Surely it was no demi-human. Perhaps a monster of some kind?* Just as he began pondering on these things, Lilula returned, a pile of dry branches under one arm and an already burning brand in the other. The maiden was humming a peaceful melody to herself and quickly set to starting a small campfire, saying nothing.

Once the pile of wood was ablaze, sparkling happily in the rock-walled valley and illuminating the large pool of water nearby, she sat down across from Jadu.

"This should warm you up in nearly no time." She offered, full of cheer.

Better illuminated by the firelight, Jadu was more fully able to determine Lilula's appearance. Her fur was mottled gray, somewhat shaggy everywhere except for around her snout, which was itself fairly short, small, and petite. Her eyes were large, one blue and one emerald, and full of spirit. Her build was average, but she was a good bit shorter than normal. Jadu guessed that if they were to stand next to each other the top of her ears would perhaps reach his chest.

He also noted two short decorative braids in her hair, one on either side of her face, that hung in front of her ears. Her ears themselves were like short, fluffy mountains atop her head. As a last matter of description, she was dressed in a high hemmed sleeveless dress of dear skin. While certainly no master of seams, Jadu was impressed with the quality of the clothing.

"Mmm… I just love warm fires on cold nights. Don't you?"

Jadu was startled by Lilula's unusually casual question.

"What? Why are you talking about such a thing?" He asked.

Lilula frowned as though thinking and scratched her ear, all the while staring into the orange flames.

"Why wouldn't I?" She finally asked in reply.

"Because… I… I do not know."

This time it was Jadu who frowned. Everything about their meeting and the current setting was wrong. But wrong in what way, he was unsure. At last, however, he landed upon an answer – Lilula was being far too kind to someone she should have only just met, while at the same time being extremely mysterious. It was unsettling, and had the distinct aura of a trap.

"Why are you helping me?" Jadu asked cautiously, hiding the distrust in his voice while testing to see if he could move his limbs. He could not.

"Um…" Lilula muttered quietly before answering. "Because."

"Because?"

"Because Mother Garnage told me to."

"Mother Garnage?"

Lilula nodded while Jadu stared at her in confusion.

"Mother Garnage is the one who raised me and taught me about the forest. I call her Mama." The maiden explained.

"Mama?" Jadu asked.

"Yes… Is that unusual?"

"I have only ever heard infants use the word. Not that I mean any offense!"

Lilula laughed, unoffended, at Jadu's sudden panic and poked at the fire with a long stick. Seeing this, Jadu quickly calmed down, and even allowed himself to relax – but only some. *She could be dangerous.* The young Pak reminded himself.

A time passed in silence, Lilula seemingly entranced with the fire, and Jadu unsure what to say. Eventually, however, the latter cleared his throat and spoke.

"Lilula,"

The maiden looked up. "Just call my Lilu." She told him.

"What?"

"Or Lula. Or Lala actually. That's what Mama calls me, Lala."

"Right… I was wondering, you say you are the one who tended my wounds, but why were you there when the battle ended? I know you are not part of my pack."

Lilula looked down at the ground as though thinking.

"I was following the black dogs." She said at last, looking back up.

"Black dogs?" Jadu asked. "You mean the Blackhounds?"

"Yes."

"Why?"

"Mother Garnage asked me to."

"Why?"

"I… I'm not allowed to tell you. Sorry."

Jadu sighed, his curiosity outridden by sudden frustration. While his thoughts collected themselves, the young Pak forced his sore limbs to move and carry him closer to the fire so he could sit down beside it.

"Who is this mother Garnage?" He asked, trying again to hide his distrust.

"She's beautiful and wise." Lilula replied, her eyes sparkling and her happiness immediately returning. "She knows all about the forest, and cares about all of the packs."

"Then why have I never heard tell of her?"

"She keeps herself hidden."

"Why?"

"…I'm not allowed to tell you. Sorry."

Jadu growled as the conversation reached another dead end.

"I'm so sorry I can't tell you more." Lilula told him, her voice sincerely apologetic. "I wish I could. But I can't."

Jadu snorted and continued to stare into the fire. This response seemed to worry the maiden, as she began to chew nervously on her hand.

"Can we still be friends?" She finally asked, the question blurting out as though water from a broken vase.

"What?" Jadu replied, surprised and, yet again, startled from his frustration.

"Is that a no? Please don't tell me that's a no." Lilula whimpered.

"Calm yourself, please. …You want to be friends?"

"…Yes?"

"We know near nothing about one another!"

Lilula frowned as though she had not realized such a thing was important and then clapped her hands excitedly and smiled a moment later.

"Ooh! Then we can talk about ourselves!" She exclaimed.

"What?" Jadu tried to ask, but he was ignored as the maiden continued to speak.

"My name is Lilula, but you can call me Lilu, Lula, or Lala. I was raised by Mama, that is, Mother Garnage. She taught me all about the forest and the animals. I like hunting and fishing and foraging. I know how to make medicines and other things from the plants and animals. I also know all the eatable plants and I make all of my own things from other things that I hunt, find, and collect. Oh! And I like pretty flowers. I really, really like pretty flowers very, very much."

Jadu stared at the maiden in confusion and surprise as she stared at him in expectation, leaning forward with her legs crossed and hands folded neatly in her lap as though a child, waiting for him to speak.

"You... You have no pack?" He finally asked.

Lilula gasped as though hurt, and then looked away.

"No." She whispered.

"Why not? What happened to them?"

The look of pain on the young woman's face intensified to the point where it seemed she might cry.

"I don't want to talk about it." She said quietly.

Jadu opened his mouth to press further, but stopped himself. This was no trick, no illusion, no trap. The hurt in Lilula's posture, voice, and eyes made that far too clear. At that moment, all doubt and mistrust in him vanished, replaced with a feeling of guilt for having reopened what was clearly a terrible scar.

"My apologies." He said. "I did not mean to hurt you."

Lilula wiped her eyes and then looked back to him, the sadness slowly fading and a smile returning.

"It's ok. What about you?"

Jadu considered resisting the question, but in the end he chose not to. She had saved his life and shared about herself, so he felt it was only fair to repay her something – however strange it was.

"My name is Jadu, I am from the Furbos pack, to the north of here. I am the son of the…"

Jadu had nearly forgot the horrible events of the day before amidst the madness of the night, but now they rushed back upon him as a devastating wave.

"…the Alpha was… my father…" He managed to say, his voice breaking.

Lilula gasped as though also remembering and then dashed from where she was sitting to be right beside the other Pak, an arm on his shoulder.

"I'm so so very very sorry!" She said. "I should have known better than to ask."

Jadu whimpered but held back his tears with his will.

"I loved… father… and mother." He said, unable to stop himself. Had he been alone he would have made the same confession.

"I'm so sorry." Lilula offered again. "I should have stayed quiet."

"It is ok." Jadu choked. "They were great people… my parents were."

"Your father… he was the Alpha? Was he the big one?"

Jadu swallowed and then nodded with a short, sad chuckle.

"He was a great warrior." Lilula consoled him. "I watched him fight with you and the others. I've never seen a living being endure so many wounds."

Jadu winced, the devastating image of his father falling to the mass of freakers striking pain into his heart. But he could discern from Lilula's voice she had said what she did as a compliment, trying to tell him how strong his father had been.

"And he was brave." The maiden continued. "Fighting so many at once. I saw that bravery in you too, when you ran after him. None of the Blackhounds you fought survived, but, if they did, I think they would never fight either of you again."

Jadu snorted, a tiny smile playing at the corners of his mouth.

"I was amazed you were still alive when you finally collapsed and the fighting was over. You had so many cuts and had lost so much blood. But your spirit and your body must be very, very strong. More so since you awoke and started running just a short time later."

Jadu finally smiled… but then sighed again as the sadness overtook him once more.

"My father said I was not ready." He confessed, giving way to his emotions and speaking to himself more than anything else. "I still do not know what he meant. Ready for what? Am I not ready as a warrior? Should I have been able to fight all of them? Am I not ready as a man? Should I have better endured losing my family? Am I not ready as a leader? For what am I not ready? No. That is a foolish question. I am ready for nothing. All of this pain has taught me that. I am ready for nothing. I am worthless."

Jadu covered his head with his hands and bowed closer to the ground.

"Worthless and weak. I failed him. I failed all of them."

Lilula opened her mouth to speak, but she knew not what to say. She moved her hand to rub the forlorn Pak's back, but she did not know if he would accept it. So, at last, she looked away, and waited.

Eventually, Jadu fell asleep – being, after all, exhausted, distraught, and weak – leaving the maiden alone in the darkness. Looking up to the stars above, she whispered a quiet prayer.

"All-King, please guide him. Amen."

Her petition asked, she looked back to the restless sleeping figure beside the dying fire. She knew exactly what his father had meant when he said he was not ready. She also knew he was most certainly *not* worthless. Her mission and her instructions from Mama remained present in her mind, but her sympathy and compassion for Jadu remained as well. Fortunately, the two were not in conflict.

Under Blackhound Hand

- a tale of Jadu, the Mighty Hound,
and Lilula, the Thunder Angel

Jadu was slow in recovering. The careless use of his injured body, coupled with the total mental and emotional collapse losing his parents and friends understandably brought upon him, resulted in this, and confined him to rest in the ravine for several days. Lilula cared for him all the while. As he healed, she hunted, cooked, and applied treatment to his wounds.

The maiden was friendly and talked regularly, not in a jabbering or caustic way at all, but, rather, quite pleasantly. She was compassionate, intelligent, humorous from time to time, willing to be quiet, and did not overstay her welcome.

At first, Jadu refused to speak back except for the barest words. But, inevitably, the persistent Lilula broke through the hastily crafted armor he had put around himself in his pain, well before it could harden, and caused him to begin talking as well. That was the evening of the second day since their encounter with the giant owl. After that, the two conversed regularly and openly.

Lilula was still secretive about any details regarding the mysterious Mother Garnage, her home, her past, or her mission. But she did share stories of woodland adventures, joyous moments she had spent in nature, and secrets she had learned along the way. Jadu, in turn, told her stories of his own life – stories of his friends and family. Every time he spoke, it is true, there was a stab at his heart that came with the memories, but the joy of sharing them was enough to push that sadness aside. Thus the young man, although unwittingly, was saved from a life of bitterness by a simple friendly presence at the right time.

Three full days passed in this manner, and then another half. At noon on that fourth day, Lilula returned from hunting to find Jadu pacing. His wounds were healed for the most, at least visibly, and he had successfully taken a walk the day before. He was ready to move again.

"I see you are feeling strong today." Lilula said happily.

The maiden set down the rabbit she had caught and began to rekindle the fire.

"I am." Jadu replied, flexing his arms and fingers to stretch out any residue of soreness.

"What do you intend to do now? Will you go home?"

Jadu shook his head. "No. I do not believe I can return there. Not now."

"Then where will you go?"

"I have pondered that myself for the last few hours since you left. I am troubled by the arrival of the Blackhounds at my home, and that we received no warning from neighboring packs. I believe I will go to some of them and seek answers."

Lilula blew on the small fire she had just resurrected and then began to fan it with her hands.

"That's easy enough." She said. "There's a Chobo village just to the east, less than a day's journey. I can show you the way."

"That is indeed a stroke of fortune."

"But I don't think you'll like what you find."

Jadu perked up his ears uncertainly. "What do you mean?"

"Well…" Lilula began nervously. "I've gotten close a few times lately and…"

"Just speak. Whatever it is."

The maiden sighed and then looked up to gaze straight into her companion's eyes.

"Blackhounds have taken control of it."

Jadu stepped back in surprise, and then growled in anger.

"And you are just telling me?" He barked.

"You needed to rest." Lilula replied, apologetic but firm, clearly not regretful of her actions. "And wounds heal fastest when calm."

"How can I be calm when Blackhounds seem to be conquering the entire world?"

"That's exactly why I didn't tell you." Lilula insisted. "Jadu, please, calm yourself. Blackhounds are on every side. They've been capturing pack after pack for the last few months. Your village was far from the first."

Jadu's eyes opened wide and his jaw dropped. *What?* The Blackhounds had been spreading like a fire for months, and no one was ever warned. How? Were there no survivors? Did they move that fast? Was it only misfortune his pack had not been reached with the news? Moreover, and the thing that angered him the most, why had Lilula kept such vital information a secret?

"How could you keep this from me?" Jadu roared.

"How did you not know it already?"

Jadu nearly collapsed. Lilula's tone and demeanor had suddenly changed to match his own, her gentle attitude breaking to reveal incredible strength beneath. The young Pak had not yet seen such force from the maiden, and was taken aback.

"I..." He stammered, startled as dumb as a boar. "How..."

40

Jadu tried to speak, but his words failed him. Lilula, in turn, glared at him for a time longer, and then sighed, her countenance immediately softening.

"I'm sorry, I shouldn't have been so harsh." She apologized. "It's not your fault you don't know what's happening around you. The Blackhound's make sure no one knows of their coming. They are fast and savage, and enslave or kill everyone in their path. Your pack is lucky to have withstood them. Most don't."

Jadu stood as though one stricken. After a time, however, his fingers curled themselves into fists, fiery rage held tight within them. He was no longer angry at Lilula. He did not know what her purpose or goal was, but it was clear enough she was benign and meant him no harm. No, he was not angry at her. He was angry at the Blackhounds. His village was attacked, his friends and family murdered, and they were not the first? Other families had been slaughtered? Other loved ones cut down? That was what enraged him.

Without a word, the man began to tramp towards the rocky wall Lilula had been using to exit the ravine. The surface was rough and easy to climb, affording a natural ladder.

"Jadu, wait." Lilula called after him, quickly putting out the fire and then following. "Where are you going?"

"I'm going to drive out the Blackhounds." He replied in a low voice that burned with vengeance.

"You can't free an entire village by yourself." The maiden argued. "You'll only be slain for nothing."

"I am determined, and I will not waver. Nothing can stop me. I swear it." Jadu declared.

"Jadu, no amount of heartfelt determination can win a war." Lilula persisted.

"But with the body of a warrior it can."

By that time, the vengeful warrior had already begun to climb the rock face, leaving his fellow Pak below. The maiden sighed and then bounded up the cliff in pursuit, quickly passing him by.

"Jadu, I admire your courage, but you need to be wise." She persisted. "Take some time to think and make a plan first, and then go."

Jadu ignored her and continued up the wall of the ravine.

"Or at least make sure your wounds won't hinder you!"

Again, the man ignored his companion and kept climbing, reaching the top a few seconds later. Lilula stood up beside him and restrained his marching away by grabbing his arm.

"Jadu, why don't we go hunting?" She suggested.

Jadu sighed and turned around, looking Lilula in the eye.

"We can make sure your body is ready for fighting again. You can stretch and warm back up. And we can have a big meal tonight." The maiden continued, her mismatched eyes sparkling with hope and just a hint of mischief. It was abundantly clear she very much liked her idea.

Jadu creased his brow and turned away.

"Jadu… please."

"No, Lilu, this is something I am going to do."

Lilula sighed and dropped her head as the foolhardy warrior headed to the east, determined to win an impossible battle. Finally, she decided to follow him, and bounded through the forest to catch up.

"At least allow me to accompany you." She insisted.

"It will be dangerous. You should not come." Jadu replied.

"Danger is supposed to scare me away but not you? That seems very hypocritical."

Jadu growled in frustration but accepted defeat.

"Can you fight?" He asked.

Lilula put a finger to her chin in thought, and then nodded.

"Yes. Mama taught me how to fight. Not with most weapons and not with skill like how you fight. But she taught me how to claw and bite and tear better than the wild animals."

Jadu remembered the scene from several days before, when he had returned to the sight of the battle – the freakers and the Blackhound witchdoctor torn to pieces. *Could it be? Could that have been her?* The Pak turned to look at his companion, who was walking contentedly beside him. He could not imagine her engaging in such violent rending of flesh, simply because of how small she was, but when he considered her personality… He did not know her well, but such a gruesome method of fighting did not seem altogether impossible.

Putting the thought aside, Jadu grunted in reluctant acceptance of the company and increased his pace; unfortunately, the trek to the Chobo village proved far more difficult than he had anticipated, and his sore limbs quickly betrayed him. However, he refused to show such "weakness" and did not slow himself to rest.

Nightfall came at last and the two made camp in a small cave. Even though the Elder Tree was now a great distance off, so far in fact that the duo need not fear its inhabitants, the threats of darkness are nothing to be trifled with.

When morning dawned, the two Pak had a small meal of herbs found nearby, and then continued their journey. In this way, they came within sight of the village well before the sun's apex, at which time

Lilula took Jadu's hand, beckoned for him to be quiet, and then led him to the top of a nearby hill. The woods around the village had been largely logged, and therefore allowed a pristine view of the town itself from atop the rise the two companions crouched on.

The settlement was small, merely an infant, so to speak, consisting of six log houses, probably one per family, and two barren scorched spots on the ground that had likely been dwellings a few weeks before. Moreover, Jadu counted no less than eight Blackhound warriors, covered in crude iron armor and carrying equally barbaric weapons, throughout both the village itself and the closely surrounding area. It was possible there were even more patrolling at a further distance.

Now, this village was just at the base of the large hill, with a stream running not far away on one side, and the forest stretching itself out in all directions. No villagers could be readily seen.

"I can likely sneak in and maybe gather some news." Lilula offered in a hushed voice. "I can climb through a window and talk to the villagers."

"Why just you?" Jadu asked in response.

The maiden looked away from the village and towards her companion, her eyes running up and down his frame once.

"Your thigh is as thick as my waist." She answered plainly.

Jadu glanced at himself and then at the Lilula. She was right, and he was not so daft as to misunderstand what she meant; *You're too big.* So instead of deny it, he resisted altogether.

"I dislike that plan." He said.

"Would you prefer to attack them directly?" Came the reply.

Now, Jadu almost answered with a simple yes, but the odds were too overwhelming, even for his vengeful spirit. Seeing his hesitation, Lilula spoke again.

"It should be easy." She said. "I can learn their patterns, patrols, and even how many of them there are from some of the villagers. And then we can make a plan. Dogs are weakest when alone, right? So it would be best to not fight them all at once."

Jadu answered with a reluctant sigh and then nodded, submitting to the wisdom. Lilula returned the sigh, hesitant to do what she had just proposed.

"Are you sure you wouldn't rather go hunting?" She asked one last time, breathless hope in her voice.

"No."

The maiden frowned at the stoic reply and puffed out a disappointed breath, like a child might do, before vanishing into the woods silently. Meanwhile, Jadu watched, staying low to the ground so he would not be spotted. He could not see Lilula, but he could see the Blackhounds – his enemies – and the villagers.

…

Lilula crept stealthily into the village, being sure to stay downwind from the Blackhound guards. Unseen, she came up alongside one of the village houses, found a window that had been opened to allow the breeze in, and then climbed through without so much as making a sound. There, just in front of her, was another woman, a few years older than herself, startled speechless.

"Don't scream." Lilula whispered to her quietly. "Please don't. I'm not here to hurt you."

The other Pak yet breathed nervously, but the fear seemed to leave her eyes – mostly.

"Who are you?" She asked in a hushed voice.

"My name is Lilula." The maiden of the forest replied. "My friend wishes to free this village. What happened here? Is there anything you can tell me that will help?"

"Nothing I'm afraid." The villager replied sadly. "And we have no one to help if it comes to a fight either. They killed all the men and older boys who didn't join them. And the ones that did join them they brought somewhere else to be 'trained'. I'm so scared for them."

The woman's eyes were wet by the time she finished speaking. A mate? A son? Both? Lilula did not know what the villager had lost, but it was clear a piece of her heart had been torn out by the Blackhounds.

"I'm so, so sorry." The maiden offered, pulling the other woman into a compassionate embrace. "But please… my friend is determined to fight. He is brave but he isn't thinking clearly. Anything at all that can help him would make me glad."

The older woman sniffled, rubbed her nose against Lilula's neck, and then separated herself from the embrace.

"There are nine Blackhounds. Four watch at any hour during the night, taking turns with the other five so they all sleep. They have spears, axes, swords, bows, arrows, and armor for their bodies and legs. Some of them have collars with spikes too."

Lilula bowed her head in appreciation.

"Is there anything else you can tell me?" She asked.

"I'm afraid not." Was the dismal answer.

Lilula bowed again and then headed for the window. Outside, atop the hill, Jadu was still watching. He had not seen her enter the building nor did he see her leave. What he did see, however, was a mother and her young daughter fetching water from the small stream, with a Blackhound guard keeping strict watch over them. Even from a distance he could tell the dark furred brute was shouting at the innocent duo and hurling harsh threats. It made his blood boil.

Jadu did not know the woman, needless to say, nor the little girl, but he could imagine he did. He knew women and girls like them from his own pack. Friends he had grown up with. Infants he had watched grow. Were they still alive? How far had the Blackhounds gone when they attacked his village? Was it only the men they killed? Or were others victims as well?

Before these thoughts had even left Jadu's mind, he found himself crouched in the brush, downwind from the woman, the child, and the Blackhound savage. He was only a few seconds of sprinting away from the fiend, and he could already feel his legs and arms tense for the pounce. He remembered nothing of moving there, nothing of stalking silently down the hill in a blind rage. He could only feel the blood writhing behind his eyes, turning his vision pink, waiting for him to avenge everything that had been taken from him!

With a growl Jadu leapt from the brush, sprinting on all fours straight towards the Blackhound. The soldier turned in surprise and drew his sword- but it was too late, already Jadu was upon him, clamping his teeth down around his throat. However, it was not flesh the crazed dog encountered, but a sharp nail, which cut into the top of his mouth. The Blackhound was wearing a spiked collar and Jadu, in his rage, had not noticed it.

Unhurt, the dark furred warrior shouted for aid and then thrust at his attacker with his blade. Jadu, in turn, tore his fangs from his foe's neck – despite the injury it caused to his mouth – and leapt away. The Blackhound attacked again, swinging for his adversary's chest, but the blow went wide. In a flash Jadu was upon him, bringing them both to the ground and pinning the warrior's sword arm.

Yips and growls echoed into the woods as the two snapped at one another's faces, bloodying their snouts. Then, suddenly, the noise turned into a scream of pain – Jadu biting down on his foe's forearm so he could rip the sword from his weakened grasp. The Blackhound howled in anger and clawed at the bigger Pak, but Jadu only leapt to his feet and thrust down with his newly claimed weapon – ending the brute's life in a single blow.

Thwack! An arrow lodged itself deeply in Jadu's back. Spinning around with a cry, the warrior saw a Blackhound archer in the woods not fifty paces from him, readying a second arrow. Beside the bowman were two more soldiers, one with a sword and the other with a spear.

Jadu growled and then charged, his anger having made him fearless. A second arrow was let fly, but this one missed altogether. Before a third could be released the other two warriors had met Jadu's mad rush, and the three collided in a frenzy of slashing chaos. Howls, yips, and growls flew through the air, along with scraps of metal, cloth, fur, and flesh.

Jadu fought with the strength and passion of a wild animal, but his training was what preserved his life. Opposing him, the Blackhounds fought with untrained savagery, and their numbers held them strong. Amidst the slashing and cleaving, Jadu could not parry or block every blow, and wounds began to appear on him. Moreover, his own attacks were kept weak by his need to defend.

Slash, slash. Nothing. The Blackhound he had assailed leapt back, and he could not follow up on his attack because of his need to spin and protect himself from the other. Slash, slash. He drove that one off as well, but then turned to do battle again with the first.

The skirmish was inevitable. Two against one, Jadu could not win. He had no armor or superior weapons to turn the tide, and the only virtues that allowed him to fight against such odds at all were his rage, superior training, and greater size and strength. But these were not enough to bring him victory, and he knew it. Therefore, he chose a different, reckless path.

No injury can strike me down! Jadu thought within himself. *I will not allow it! My vengeance will be satiated only when every Blackhound pays with blood! Death cannot stop me! I refuse!*

With a shouting roar, Jadu leapt upon one of his two foes, slashing and hacking like a rabid creature! The Blackhound fearfully defended, his eyes wide with terror for his life, but it was done and over in only a second, and the soldier fell dead.

Unfortunately, the mad attack was not without cost. Jadu had indeed pressed his assault, and indeed he had struck down one of his foes, but his other enemy's spear now protruded from his abdomen, thrust straight through him from behind.

He knew that was going to happen. He did not care. He lifted his sword, turned to face the spearmen and… no, that is not right. He was not moving. Why was he not moving? Jadu looked down at the spearhead erupting from his stomach and tried to turn around. It did not hurt, why could he not turn?

Irritated by the object, the young Pak lifted his hand to the tip and grasped hold of it, trying to push it back out. The spear moved willingly, pulled free by the spearmen himself, cutting Jadu's fingers.

Now Jadu was on the ground. Why? Had he fallen? How could he fall? He was so angry. Was that rage not enough to sustain him? Rolling onto his back, Jadu looked up at the Blackhound standing over him – and stabbed him in the leg with his sword… No? His sword did not move. Why?

Crack! The Blackhound screamed a dying cry and then collapsed to the ground in a smoking heap, slain by an unseen attack. Suddenly, Lilula was kneeling over Jadu, holding his face and checking him for life. The warrior was covered from head to toe in claw marks, bite wounds, and cuts. The worst injury was most certainly the one in his stomach from the spear, but several others came close. How had he not noticed them?

"I told you to wait." The maiden scolded her battered companion.

Jadu muttered something that could not be understood in response, just before his eyes rolled back in his skull and his breathing began to slow.

"Jadu? Jadu? Wake up."

Lilula shook the crippled mess that was Jadu and tried to arouse him, even though she knew it would be to no avail. She had seen dead animals ravaged by weather and scavengers that appeared more alive than the big Pak lying before her; yet still he clung to his mortality – however weakly.

Looking frantically around, the maiden saw nothing but the dead bodies of the Blackhounds – two slain by her and two by Jadu – and the mother with her child, huddled together in fear some several paces away. The remaining Blackhounds were likely waiting at the village for some form of report. After all, they knew not that the sounds of battle they had heard were from but one man's resistance. As far as they were aware, an entire army could be circling around them in preparation for an attack. It was that uncertainty that gave Lilula just the time she needed.

After clogging her companions wounds with soil to slow the bleeding, the maiden reached into a small bag – no larger than a man's fist – on her hip and took from it an intricately carved wooden instrument shaped something like a conch shell. Next, she lifted the strange object to her lips, and blew into one end, making a sound similar to an animal's bray.

After maintaining a solid note for several seconds, Lilula lowered the instrument from and put it back into her bag.

"Please be nearby, Tips." She begged quietly into the woods as she looked nervously about for any new threats.

Beside the maiden, Jadu muttered something once more. Turning to the fallen warrior, she took one of his hands in hers and folded it across his chest, clutching it tight.

"It'll be ok you stupid oaf." She told him gently, even though she doubted he could hear her. "You can survive this."

Just then, a nearby bush rustled. Lilula's open hand shot up with claws out in case she needed to fight, her eyes darting to the sound. But such fear 'twas not necessary, and the maiden quickly sighed in relief, letting her guard down at the same time.

Out of the woods trotted a majestic elk, very peculiar in appearance. Not only was he larger than most other elk by a good five hands, and crowned with antlers bespeaking impressive age, but his fur was as white as snow, and his eyes as red as sunset. This was Lilula's old friend, whom she had lovingly named Tips.

Locking his scarlet eyes on the two Pak, the great albino creature walked regally out of the brush and then knelt before Lilula, bowing his head and braying quietly. The maiden, in turn, took hold of one of his antlers gently and pulled their foreheads together, smiling as she did so.

"Thank you." She whispered. "I knew you would follow me."

With that, she released her grasp on the beast and immediately stood.

"I'm sorry," She said. "but I need your help."

Without another word she crouched down behind Jadu and began to lift him as best she could, her small size and his impressive bulk working directly against each other. However, after several seconds and much panting, she was finally able to "roll" her companion across the mighty elk's back so that he hung across it like a saddlebag. After seating herself just behind Jadu and adjusting his weight so he would not easily fall off, the maiden patted Tips's neck, and the beast obediently stood up.

Looking around once more for danger, Lilula put one hand on her unusual steed's shoulder and the other on Jadu's back to support him, and then led them quickly into the woods. Just before she disappeared into the forest though, she looked back to the frightened mother and child, who were silently watching her with large, fearful eyes.

"I'm so, so, very very sorry." She told them. "I promise. We will be back to free you."

With that, she turned back to the woods and vanished into the shadows, along with the elk, and the wounded Jadu. Looking into one of the brave, foolish Pak's mostly closed eyes, Lilula sighed deeply within herself.

"We will be back," She whispered. "as soon as this one realizes he is *not* ready."

The Spring of the Great Tree
- a tale of Lilula, the Thunder Angel

Lilula had traveled far for but one day's trek, watching the crippled form of Jadu sway on Tips's, the white elk's, back with every step. She had no fear of pursuit: she had covered their tracks well. But she did fear if her injured companion could long hold to his fleeting life – the crimson stains on Tips's ivory coat a stolid reminder of the warrior's grim condition…

When evening had come, the maiden took Jadu from Tips's back and hid him in a natural den, formed between a large rock and a fallen tree. His breathing was weaker now than it had been, and despite the bandages she had applied to his wounds, he had lost much blood.

As Lilula busied herself with her wounded friend, Tips brayed, walked a short distance, and then lay down in exhaustion. Hearing this happen, the young Pak quickly left Jadu's side, ran to the elk, and lovingly embraced the grand beast despite his dirtied fur.

"Thank you so much, Tips." She said. "You had a lot to carry for a long time. You did wonderfully."

The noble creature mewed happily and then set his head down and closed his eyes to sleep. Lilula, for her part, squeezed him tightly for a few more seconds, stood up, patted him once more on the neck, and then turned to look again at Jadu. The rise and fall of the other Pak's chest was so labored and slight it was hard to watch, and she feared if he would make it through the night. No. She knew he would not – not even with all his bravery and natural vigor. But that was why she had brought him to that specific place.

Turning, Lilula looked up towards one of the five Elder Trees that dotted their island home of Tarfa, no more than two miles distant, standing like a stalwart monolith of ancient times. Sunset was nearly past, and the most dangerous time to be about was fast approaching. Traveling at night, alone especially, was dangerous, but approaching an Elder Tree during those killing hours… for any normal man or woman, such was madness.

But Lilula had not been raised as a farmer or a seamstress, or with any other such common occupation. Had she not been raised in nature by the wise Mother Garnage? Had she not been taught all the secrets of the forest and how to avoid or overcome any obstacle she might face in the woodland realm? Was she not the one who had led Jadu safely away from the giant owl? The one who could have killed the beast if she so wished?

Now, 'tis true that even for her the path to the tree was dense with peril. But Jadu had too little time left, and his wounds were too severe to be cured with simple herbs and bandages. If anything was going to save him, it would be water from the spring at the base of *that* specific Elder Tree. Imbued with the power of the great tree, the waters from that spring could cure nearly any ill without so much as a word nor any preparation. Lilula had seen its power herself. She knew it could save the injured man behind her. All she had to do was retrieve it.

The maiden breathed deeply to ready herself… and then set off at a shallow run, time itself her enemy.

…

Giant owls flew overhead, unable to catch their prey because of the skill with which it dodged between and under the massive roots of the Elder Tree. Titanic snakes remained asleep and undisturbed by the stealthy trespasser. Enormous spiders watched as well, joined with all manner of other creatures terrifying for their size and power.

For a mile and more around the base of the Elder Tree, it was as though the world had grown. Animals, insects, and plants were larger and more vibrant. But, amongst all that, Lilula was still her normal, small, self.

What did she care though? Her size made it easier to evade the unnaturally large predators; to fit beneath the Elder Tree's roots and between the stems of giant flowers. It meant her scent was harder to detect, and her enemies were all the easier to see. As the small one, she had the advantage in stealth that she did not need in strength.

And so, the maiden soon arrived at the base of the tree, two of its enormous roots forming something akin to the walls of a large room round about. Before her lay a spring of crystal-clear water, resting perfectly still in the darkness; part of it beneath the great trunk and part of it without.

That "trunk" was at least a thousand paces around, as large as some castles and certainly larger than most forts. Those "roots" were as tall as two or three men atop one another's shoulders, and covered in bark as thick and strong as plated armor, which was yet somehow thinner than the covering for the rest of the tree.

Lilula paid no heed to these incredible things though. They were normal to her after all. Instead, she stepped tenderly out of the bush she was hiding in, and looked about as though trying to find someone.

"Keeper?" She called quietly into the darkness, her hushed voice echoing for lack of any other noise.

Suddenly, out of the silence came a sound like leaves rustling together, then like wood cracking under strain, then, in a flash of light, a man appeared between Lilula and the spring of water! Now, I say "man", but that is a misguiding statement. The being that thus appeared was nearly twice the height of any normal human or Pak, and made of wood. His proportions were thick but somehow also long. A beard of moss flowed from his face down across his chest, and long hair of the same fell around his shoulders. When he opened his eyes, they glimmered an impossibly brilliant green in the darkness, illuminated by some strange light from within.

Lilula found herself resisting the urge to tremble as she bowed her head politely before the incredible figure.

"Why have you come?" The "man" asked with a booming, shattering voice befitting of his appearance.

Lilula bowed deeper.

"Great Keeper," She said. "I humbly beg a few drops from the tree's spring."

The reply was immediate and spoken without hesitation.

"No."

Lilula swallowed. She had expected rejection to be his first answer. However, she had more to say, and so she spoke again, her head still bowed respectfully.

"Sir. I am Lilula, the surrogate daughter of Mother Garnage, your sister Keeper. I make this request so that I might fulfil a duty she has given to me."

"You are Garnage's welp?"

The rhetorical question was asked into silence, and for several seconds, not so much as a breath broke the eerie quiet. At last, however, the one Lilula had called "Keeper" spoke again.

"I see. I can indeed sense her on you. Yet my answer remains the same. 'Tis the duty of the Keepers to guard the Elder Trees and all of their mysteries. If Garnage wishes to defile her sacred responsibility by adopting a savage mortal wench, that is her choice. If it goes too far she will be replaced, although that is not my place to say. But enough of this nonsense – why do I explain immortal affairs to a child? Your 'Mother' may be compassionate, but I am not. Begone!"

Thus rebuked, Lilula bit her tongue to restrain herself from shouting back in indignation, offended both for herself and for the one who raised her. Yay, instead or returning insult for insult, the maiden kept her head bowed, knowing full well what had just been spoken was meant to offend her. She still had one last reason she could offer in exchange for the boon that would save Jadu's life.

"The one I need the water for is the Serpent's Heir." She explained, her voice frighteningly calm after what had just been said to her.

The Keeper stood as though struck. Five. Six. Seven. Eight seconds passed in absolute silence before the strange man finally stirred himself as if waking from a dream.

"Explain." He demanded.

"This one has endured the venom of the Great Snake." Lilula said, holding back her anxiety. "He has survived the toxin, and even now its power courses through his veins. You know, doubtlessly, good Keeper, what this means; That if we are to save Tarfa from the Blackhounds, he is the only one who can do it."

The Keeper contemplated the Pak maiden before him with sharp eyes for a time, and then crossed his arms before stating his decree.

"The answer remains: no."

Lilula's head shot up in surprise and she could not resist shouting out.

"But the fate of all Tarfa relies on it!"

"All of the *Pak* rely on it." The Keeper replied heartlessly. "But that is not my duty nor my concern. I will protect this tree, all of its secrets, and the tunnels beneath it from any race and any tribe. Even from one sent by my sister Keeper."

Lilula gasped in disbelief. She could see the wooden man was determined though, so she sighed and closed her eyes. *I tried.* She thought. *...I tried the peaceful option.* Lifting her eyes, the maiden stood up tall before the towering Keeper, and showed respectful defiance – her head unbowed and her eyes sharper than even his.

"Keeper, I am sorry, but I will be leaving here with the water I requested." She declared.

"Are you dare threatening me?" The oaken giant demanded, anger seeping out with the words.

"No. I wish you no harm and bear you no grudge." Lilula replied. "But Mother Garnage commanded me that if I were to find the Serpent's Heir, I was to protect his life at all costs, barring he was not evil at heart. She told me plainly that I was even to resist herself, or any other Keeper who hindered that purpose. Dragons, demons, armies, and false gods are amongst those I promised her I would oppose if necessary, and so are you. So please, I beg of you, step aside. This need not come to blows."

"Insolent wretch." The Keeper growled, making his decision clear. "You can die where you stand!"

There was the sudden sound of earth being ripped up and plants moving as an army of vines rushed out of the dirt and towards Lilula! The maiden closed her eyes as though in acceptance but – at the last moment – she opened them again, wind surging around her as though an infant storm had been released from within her bosom. The vines were repelled, thrown back to crash against the roots of the tree.

Seeing this, the Keeper began to speak out in surprise, but before he could utter even a single word, Lilula stretched out both hands, and lightning flashed forth from her palms – her forearms cackling with white power, their bones glowing through flesh and fur. True to its destructive nature, the arcing light blasted the stubborn protector of the tree and dropped him to the ground with a final cry: nothing but a smoking heap.

After the short-lived conflict, Lilula remained still for a few seconds, panting heavily, with her arms shaking and her knees buckling.

The vines lay limp where they had been thrown by the wind, and the Keeper did not stir. With a sigh, the maiden finally relaxed and lowered her arms. However, the urgency of her mission quickly returned to her mind, and she rushed past the fallen guardian to the glimmering spring of life-giving water.

Kneeling by the side of the pool, the young Pak took her waterskin from her side, drank the last few drops from it, wiped its mouth, and then dipped it into the clear spring. As soon as she had taken what she needed to heal Jadu, she withdrew the skin, sealed the cap, and turned to leave.

Just then, vines shot out of the ground and entangled her! Wrapping around her arms, legs, wrists, ankles, throat, stomach, chest, and muzzle. She was completely restrained in but a fraction of a second! And there, standing before her, was the Keeper, burnt to coal. Yet, as the maiden watched, the giant being's blackened "skin" and charred beard revived as strong wooden flesh and vibrant moss, his eyes gleaming with wrath.

With but a few steps, the outraged defender came to an arm's reach of Lilula and snatched the waterskin from her hand. No words were spoken as he then walked past the imprisoned maiden and to the spring.

Behind him, the vines around the young Pak's chest and throat were tightening, slowly strangling her as she struggled to free herself.

The Keeper ignored her though, and dumped out the water she had taken. Drip drip drip. Less than a mouthful of the crystal fluid emerged from the skin and rejoined the pool it had come from... The Keeper stood frozen. Lilula still struggled to escape behind him, but her throes were becoming weak as want for air caused her head to throb and her limbs to become numb.

"That is it?" The Keeper asked, his voice nothing more than an astonished whisper. "Nothing but a swallow?"

Turning, he looked at Lilula's nearly limp form, and then swept his hand to the side as though ordering the vines to retreat. The foliage obeyed, and the maiden was dropped to the ground, panting for breath. When she at last opened her eyes and looked up some several seconds later, she saw the Keeper holding her waterskin – now filled with water from the crystal spring – out to her.

"Take it." The giant said unhappily. "You have proven your respect and honesty – the truth of your heart. If you will risk your life so willingly for this mission given to you by my sister Keeper, and ask so little of me, then fine: take it quickly, before my mind is changed."

Lilula panted in a few more ragged breaths, and then bowed her head respectfully.

"Thank you... great Keeper." She said.

"Thank me by taking your boon and leaving." The guardian replied sternly.

The young Pak rose shakily to her feet, accepted the waterskin gratefully, and then turned to depart.

…

Tips was gone by the time Lilula returned to Jadu, but the wounded Pak himself was still lying in the den where she had left him. At first, approaching, as she was, in the darkness, the maiden feared she was too late, and he had already perished. But then his chest rose ever so faintly as he took a fleeting breath, and Lilula's hope rekindled.

Immediately she snuggled herself into the den beside him and took the waterskin from her hip. Opening it carefully, she tilted back Jadu's head and slowly poured the precious water into his mouth, taking heed not to choke him. The wounded Pak swallowed reflexively in his restless sleep, but otherwise made no motion.

This done, Lilula returned the skin to her side, and then lay down as far away from Jadu as she could in the small space. Finally, as one last measure before retiring for the night, she prayed to the All-King that the water would save the life of the man beside her, and that she had made no mistakes in her conduct that day. This short prayer concluded, the maiden of the forest closed her eyes, and fell into an uneasy slumber.

...

The next morning, Lilula awoke to the sound of Jadu panicking. Opening her eyes slowly, she rolled over and looked at him to try and find out what the matter was: he was pressed as tightly as he could be against the opposing wall of the den and stammering on his words.

Still uncertain, Lilula yawned, stretched, and then smacked her lips to moisten them.

"What's wrong?" She asked, rubbing the sleep from her eyes.

"Why are we in the same den?" Jadu finally managed to ask. "What happened? Am I not dead?"

Lilula looked at her companion in confusion for a time, and then grasped at his reasoning – he remembered nothing since his battle with the Blackhounds. Sleeping so close to each other, of course, was not the problem; tight bed arrangements are common for Pak. But wait...? Was that only for Pak of the same pack? Lilula, admittedly, did not know. Had she done something strange?

Putting the thought aside for a moment, the maiden crawled out of the den and then turned around so she could face Jadu.

"I'm sorry." She said. "Did I do something wrong sleeping so close to you?"

Jadu sighed at the other Pak's words and seemed to finally regain control of himself.

"No, of course not." He replied apologetically. "I was simply not expecting it."

Lilula smiled at the answer and then crouched down to offer Jadu a hand.

"How are you feeling?" She asked.

The bigger Pak accepted the aid in exiting the den and then stood up somewhat stiffly.

"I feel fine." He told her. "A bit sore, but otherwise unhurt. But... I thought for sure... Did I not...?"

Lilula scratched at her arm nervously before answering Jadu's unspoken question.

"You were nearly killed." She said. "I got you away, and then healed you with a special... medicine... of sorts."

Jadu held out his arms in front of him and began to look himself over.

"You are capable of such a thing?" He asked in awe.

"No!" Lilula replied quickly. "Or... I mean... not really. I used a special water. It is awfully hard to get and I have no more of it."

Jadu finished looking at himself and then turned back to her.

"I see no scars." He said. "Nothing remains of any wounds I obtained. Your healing water must be incredible. I am sorry you had to waste it on a fool like me."

Lilula hid a gasp of surprise. How should she respond to such a thing? He certainly had been a fool, it was true, but she did not at all consider saving him a waste.

"It was no waste." She declared, sticking to the truth. "No matter how much a fool you were, I still believe in what you can become."

"That is… a strange thing to say." Jadu replied.

"Oh… yes… I suppose it is." The maiden mumbled, turning away as she realized her companion did not know the same things as she.

After that, a few seconds passed in silence, until – *thump*. Jadu had fallen back against the large rock that formed part of the den, and slid to the ground, holding his head in his hands.

"Jadu?" Lilula asked, turning back to him. "Are you certain you are alright?"

"I accomplished nothing." The man lamented in response. "I remember little of the battle… I was so consumed with rage and a need for justice that I lost control. But even with all my anger, all my training, and all my determination, I could not save even a single person. What is worse, I needed saving myself."

Lilula walked over to the brave, distraught Pak and sat down beside him, nuzzling his arm with her nose.

"You learned from it though." She reminded him. "The pain has sealed a truth into your heart that you won't forget, not in a thousand years."

"And what truth is that?" Jadu asked.

"The one your father tried to teach you. That you aren't ready." Was the answer.

The big Pak's muscles tensed suddenly as though in anger, but just as quickly relaxed.

"I already knew that. Ever since… that day… I knew I was not ready to be the man my father wanted." He said.

Lilula understood full well that Jadu knew he was lying to himself, and waited in silence for his own confession. She believed, rightly, he was honest enough to see it without her aid.

"No… That is not true. I only convinced myself I had failed and it was my fault I had lost them." He said. "It was not humility, only guilt and sadness."

Lilula rubbed her nose against Jadu's neck to comfort him, and he replied by scratching the back of her head – not at all strange for Pak.

"Pride is all consuming." The maiden said. "If you believe you don't need to change you won't. True men, and women, look first to how they can be better, then they look upon the rest of the world."

As his companion spoke, Jadu gazed towards the ground with a few tears in his eyes.

"That is what father was trying to tell me!" He exclaimed once she finished. "That the only way I would ever be ready would be to know I am not. I was too proud! I had long stopped seeing flaws in myself as something to be removed, but just as another part of who I was. I had ceased to grow, to change, to become better. I believed I was already 'ready'. Under the guise of 'accepting who I was' I believed I was perfect. I was such a fool." Jadu lifted his eyes to the treetops, trying to see the sky through the leafy canopy. "Lilula, thank you."

"Mmmh."

…The man could but blink in surprise at the strange response, and then turn to look toward the maiden beside him: Lilula had her eyes closed and mouth open as she leaned her head into his fingers. Seeing this, Jadu stopped scratching.

"What?" The young woman asked as she opened her eyes slowly. "Oh! Sorry. I heard everything you said. It was very humble. Oh! – and you're welcome."

The stammered jumble of words was followed by two dramatically different, although expected, responses: Jadu laughed hysterically as Lilula turned away in embarrassment, pretending to be distracted with a nearby rock. A need to defend herself quickly arose within the maiden, however, and she did so with all her might.

"I don't get scratches very often, alright!" She blurted out, as though it were an excuse. "I'm not used to it and I get carried away!"

Far from stopping Jadu's laughter, the uncharacteristically pathetic defense only caused him to laugh all the harder. If Lilula were a human, her face would have been crimson. Therefore, indignant with her own – ironically – pride offended, she turned her snout away, into the air, and crossed her arms.

Jadu finally finished laughing several seconds later and wiped a few tears of mirth from his eyes.

"My apologies." He said. "I meant no offense, Lilula."

Lilula harrumphed the apology and kept her nose raised, but her eyes had secretly opened and her lips were quivering in self condemnation of her haughty attitude. Before she could compose an appropriate response, though, she felt something touch the back of her head.

"Jadu what are you-?" She started to ask, but was cut short by her own delighted sigh as her companion began scratching behind her ear.

"You're being cruel…" She complained quietly, trying to hide her embarrassment but at the same time unwilling to resist.

"Just consider it payment for saving my life." Jadu replied.

Accepting the suggestion, Lilula finally relaxed, and leaned into her companion's fingers again.

"Fine. But just this once."

The Laughing Hunt

- a tale of Jadu, the Mighty Hound,
and Lilula, the Thunder Angel

Most stories of heroes are filled with courage, daring, and noble deeds. This is no such story – at least not to the degree of many another tale I have told. But I tell this tale no less, for it is worthwhile. The moral is simple: sometimes 'tis good to have fun. There will ever and always be another battle to fight and another struggle to drudge through, but once and again a moment of mirth is to be enjoyed. Even heroes need rest. And sometimes, as with this story, that rest can be quite entertaining for us lot. Hoho. Let us begin.

…

"Let's go hunting!"

That was the first sound Jadu heard on the morning after the one on which he had awoken healed. Opening his eyes, he saw Lilula's mismatching gaze staring down at him, one eye forest green and the other ocean blue – but both sparkling with excitement.

With a groan the man sat up, his companion moving out of the way as he did so.

"Why?" He asked sleepily.

"You've had a full day to recover." Lilula answered. "And since we tried to rescue the village last time like you wanted, it's time to do what I wanted."

The duo exited the makeshift den they had slept in, thus allowing Jadu to stand up and stretch.

"Are you that excited to hunt together?" He asked.

67

"Yes." Lilula replied most simply. "But it'll also be good for you."

"How?"

"You'll see. Anyways, let us be off!"

The maiden threw a bow at Jadu and then turned and began marching into the woodland. Jadu caught the bow and followed but, just then, his stomach growled ravenously.

"Do we have any food?" He asked from behind as Lilula lead the way.

"Nope." Was the answer. "Another benefit to the hunting."

"I suppose that is only fair. Did you make these bows yourself?"

Lilula spun around so she was facing Jadu, and took to walking backwards as she smiled and talked.

"Yes I did." She beamed proudly. "I spent all of yesterday gathering the parts and putting them together."

Jadu did not respond with words, but instead held up the weapon he had been given and ran his eyes along its surface. It was crude, truly, but he did not doubt its effectiveness – five or six sturdy seedlings bound together by stout creepers, and a thick thread connecting the two ends. The entirety of the body was so thick he could scarcely hold it in a single hand. Therefore the power behind it must have been incredible!

Lilula's bow, in contrast, was much thinner, consisting of only two thick seedlings with a thread attaching the two ends. Jadu also noticed a bundle of nine or ten wooden arrows on the maiden's back, long and sharpened to a deadly point.

"Come on." Lilula urged, having turned back to her path and increased in speed.

Jadu began jogging to keep up.

"Wyverns don't normally live this far south, but there's a mountain not far away where a cove of them nest." The maiden told him.

"Wyverns!" Jadu exclaimed.

"Is that so surprising?"

"I thought we were hunting deer or elk!"

"Why, when Wyverns taste so much better?"

"Because I fear fire breath, talons, and poisoned fangs!"

"No concern if you know how to hunt them properly."

"I do not!"

"I'll teach you then."

Lilula skipped backwards a few steps until she was beside Jadu, and then continued to guide their path from next to her companion. She could tell from his eyes he was frightened. But why? Were wyverns truly that dreadful?

"It's not dangerous if you do it right." Lilula said again. "Wyverns have very good eyes and noses, but they can't hear half as good as a grandmother skunk. So the first rule is to stay downwind from them and avoid anywhere they could see you. Being quiet is good but as long as you aren't loud they won't hear you."

Jadu nodded in understanding, but his jaw was tight. Despite this, Lilula decided to keep going.

"Now, their scales are tough and wyverns themselves are big, so you can't shoot at them like you would something with hooves. Their main weak spot is their eyes, which are big like a snake's, so they're easy to hit. The trick is to get really really close without them noticing you, and then don't miss. One arrow of this length through the eye ought to kill any normal wyvern. If it doesn't: run."

Jadu nodded again.

"And what if they do notice us and attack?" He asked.

"Run." Lilula replied (unknowingly) in the most uncomforting way possible. "And don't swerve! That's just stupid. They're too big and too agile, they'll just kill you anyways. Your only way to escape is to run as fast as you can and get to some sort of cover."

"So then there is no way to fight them at all?" Jadu inquired.

The question was apparently not as simple as the bigger Pak had assumed, as Lilula put a finger to her chin and tapped it in thought.

"Well…" She began after a bit of contemplation. "that's not entirely true: you *can* fight them, and I have done so before. But with our weapons that would be closer to tempting the All-King's goodness than being brave."

"Regardless," Jadu replied. "I would like to know how."

"Ok." The maiden conceded happily as they continued on their trek. "Wyverns have a few main weapons you need to concern yourself with. First is their fangs and teeth. They have teeth like a lizard but also fangs like a serpent. The teeth will break your bones and rip you to shreds but they aren't venomous. The fangs are venomous. But wyverns are big enough that if they get a fang into you, you should be more concerned with the fang itself than the venom."

Jadu nodded.

"Next is their tail. They use their tail like a whip. They don't slash or wrap or grapple with it against smaller things like us, they just whip it. On the end of the tail is a crescent shaped claw that can cut through even tough leather. One hit and you're probably dead."

Again, Jadu nodded grimly. Lilula, however, carried on as though having a casual conversation.

"Last is the fire breath. They don't use it very much, especially against us. Teeth and tail are their favorites, their fire is more like a final option if nothing else is working. Fortunately for us, it's easy to dodge. When they start making a weird hissing-cackling sound, that means they're about to roast you. That's when you swerve."

"This is all good to know." Jadu interrupted. "But it does not tell me how to *fight* them in the slightest."

"I was almost to that part." Lilula resumed. "It's not hard, but it *is* very risky. You see, wyverns have eyes like a bird's, meaning they can't see anything right in front of their face. That's key. If you can get it to turn its head to look at you, then you stab it in the eye. At that point it goes crazy and starts flailing around while you run and hope you don't get killed by the flapping talons and claws."

"Wonderful…"

"But, to get to that point, you do this: first, if it gets close enough you're going to fight it, go straight for the blind spot right at the front of its nose. When it loses sight of you, it will try to bite your head since it knows you're in front of it. At that point, jump to the side and ready your weapon – in this case, an arrow – in the same hand as the direction you dodged.

"Next, when it sees you have escaped its teeth, it will whip its tail at you. You're already moving, so just arc your body and twist at the last second. They almost always whip at the chest, so if you twist right it will go right past you. Then, before it pulls its tail back for another whip or turns its head: stab it in the eye. After all, it's been staring at you to know where to aim its tail."

Lilula concluded her lesson by taking a few hopping steps forward, leaping onto a nearby log, and then turning to look at Jadu happily with her hands on her hips.

"Easy." She declared.

Jadu, however, was not convinced, and groaned into his hands while wondering why he had not yet turned tail and fled.

…

About midday, while yet a few hours from the hunting grounds, the two travelers happened across a cluster of large berry bushes in full bloom, heavy with their bounty.

"These are safe to eat!" Lilula exclaimed in excitement upon seeing them. "Let's stop here for lunch! We can eat some berries and fill up our water at that brook over there."

Jadu stopped walking with a tired huff and slumped his shoulders in unspoken agreement. He was tired and hungry – lunch sounded like a splendid idea.

And so, after leaning on a tree for a few seconds to catch his breath, Jadu began to pick and eat the berries willingly. Under normal circumstances he would have preferred some form of meat, but having not eaten all that day he was much more tolerant.

Thwack. Something hard bounced off of his temple.

"What?"

Thwack. A second object hit him.

Lifting a hand defensively, Jadu turned in the direction of the attack. Thwack. A berry bounced off of his knuckle.

"Lilula!"

The maiden giggled elfishly at the (correct) accusation and then threw another berry at her companion. Jadu, in turn, ducked and threw one back.

"Stop it." He said.

Lilula paused at the demand, looked up towards the sky and tapped her chin as she often did when deep in thought, and then shook her head.

"No."

Thwack thwack thwack.

"Ow."

Jadu ducked behind a tree, rubbing his eye – which had just been hit – while the wily Lilula laughed relentlessly. Once recovered, the man growled in annoyance, picked a berry, and then threw it at the maiden as hard as he could.

…

"Why is there a nest of wyverns this far south?" Jadu asked.

The two Pak had been walking uphill for quite a distance, but by that time the steepness had come to such a point that the duo was frequently clambering up rocky slopes.

"You made it sound as if they only live to the north." The man finished saying.

"Well, this isn't a normal nesting sight." Lilula replied as they continued to climb. "Some of the younger males come here to hunt and 'train' until a female comes looking for a mate. It's similar to a wyvern bachelor camp."

"What?" Jadu demanded in disbelief. "My apologies, I fear I must not have heard you perfectly. You said we are going to hunt young, cocky, *male*, wyverns who will probably be more violent than usual because they are young, cocky, male wyverns trying to attract a mate and intimidate any challengers."

"Exactly." Lilula answered with a laugh in her voice. "I doubt they'll even recognize you're not from their group."

Jadu rolled his eyes before responding.

"You are making this sound less dangerous than it is." He said. "The only comfort you have given regarding this hunt is 'if you make even a single mistake: you die'."

Lilula laughed.

"I seem to remember you singlehandedly attacking multiple Blackhound warriors at one time, *without* a plan."

"I suppose it is fair to bring that up." Jadu grumbled. "However, if I perished there at least it would have been for a noble cause. But for this? What would I have died for? Some meat, a good story, and perhaps a grand trophy?"

"Of course not. Don't be ridiculous." Lilula answered. "We're not doing this for meat, and trophies are nothing but vanity. We're doing this because it's fun."

The unexpected declaration was so surprising that Jadu choked on his own tongue and nearly fell off the boulder he and Lilula were scaling. Fortunately, however, he kept his grip and quickly caught his breath.

"Fun!" He exclaimed.

"Yes, fun." Lilula replied. "If we wanted meat we could hunt something a lot easier to get to. This is for the experience, the story, the memories."

"Have you no fear for your life woman?"

This time it was Lilula who rolled her eyes.

"Of course I do." She said. "But I am not afraid now because I know we will be safe. I have done this before, after all. The first time I killed a wyvern I was only twelve years of age. Naturally, I believe you can be at least as capable and brave as a little girl." Lilula reached the top of the boulder and offered Jadu a hand. "Am I wrong?"

The bigger Pak accepted the aid, climbed the rest of the way up, and then replied while gazing upon the next portion of cliff they would be scaling.

"You are not wrong." He conceded. "I will be brave. But still… I see no purpose to this."

Lilula put her toes and fingers to the next slope and began picking her way up the rocky surface.

"You will." She said confidently. "There's a future ahead of you that I don't believe you see yet. And in that future you will need experiences and memories like these to look back on and draw strength from. This *will* be a good thing for you. I truly believe that, and wouldn't be pressing you so if I didn't."

The maiden paused to look back at her companion, who had also begun climbing.

"Do you trust me?" She asked.

Jadu looked up at her and hesitated before answering.

"You have given me no reason not to." He confessed. "So, yes, I suppose I do."

Lilula bowed her head in thanks.

"I appreciate it, Jadu. I promise not to betray that trust."

In this manner, the two Pak continued up the side of the rocky woodland mountain; sometimes walking, sometimes climbing. As a note, wyverns hunt mostly at night, and only rarely during the day. Moreover, Lilula, of course, knew this, and shared that comfort with Jadu so that they could progress with minimal fear. And so time passed.

Late that afternoon, the adventure began in earnest. The duo had just finished climbing a steep cliffside – the forest stretching out like a map beneath them by then – and were making their way through a copse of trees when Lilula suddenly froze and put her hand out for Jadu to do the same. The man obeyed.

…Nothing moved. Not so much as a breeze shook the leaves. But then, distantly, there was a strange moan-like roar. Hearing it, Jadu swallowed.

"Wyvern." Lilula declared quietly beside him, her voice shaking with excitement.

Jadu took in a deep breath and then nodded to show her he had heard. In contrast to his apprehension, the maiden merely smiled and handed him some of the arrows before leading the way towards the sound. A short while later, they came to the edge of the tree-line and looked out onto a wide, rocky clearing perhaps fourscore paces square. On the far side of this plateau was a stream that flowed out from the side of the mountain, bubbled across the platform, and then cascaded downward in a large waterfall.

The concept of the location was this: From where Jadu and Lilula stood, the mountain was to their left, a cliff was to their right, and the stream was on the opposite end of the clearing. Directly in the center of the clearing, halfway between the two hunters and the stream, was a wyvern.

The frightful creature appeared at least large enough to devour a horse, possessing a broad, strong chest, thick neck, draconic head, powerful legs, sizeable talons, a thrashing tail at least two men in length, and massive batlike wings in place of forelegs.

Jadu sized up the beast from where he hid in the brush. By his best guess its head was a bit larger than an average man's body, and its fangs as long as a short-sword. If size alone were not enough, the claws on the ends of its wings, toes, and tail left no doubts in regard to its lethal capability.

Now, as a matter of clarification before continuing: the beast thus described is a Northern Wyvern, native to colder lands. Southern Wyverns differ from their hardy cousins, but that is another tale.

"This is madness." Jadu whispered. "Such a beast is too mighty for us two."

"Just be brave." Lilula answered him, her voice reassuring even though her patience was thin by that time. "It's even hurt. This will be easy."

What the maiden spoke was true. The creature was lying alone, in the middle of the clearing, exposed to the sun, with its wings spread out to reveal large bloody wounds all across them. Seeing this, Jadu easily recognized the universal signs of a fight between males – either over food or a mate.

While he pondered on these things, Lilula had already crept out of the trees and was stealthily approaching the beast, an arrow knocked and ready. Because the wyvern's eyes were closed and its breathing was labored, the maiden took few precautions on her approach, trusting her trained senses to warn her in case of danger. On the other hand, Jadu noticed his companion's absence only after a brief delay, whereupon he quickly moved to catch up, getting his own bow and arrows ready.

At twenty paces, the wyvern lifted its head and opened its eyes halfway, looking all around itself. Suddenly, its eyes opened wide and it stared sideways at the two Pak, who had frozen not too far distant.

Jadu swallowed his fear, trying not to be paralyzed by that massive eye staring him down. Even Lilula took a deep, quiet breath before continuing to creep forward.

The beast gazed straight upon the Pak.

The maiden drew back the string of her bow.

The wyvern cocked its head as though trying to see her better, locking its slit-like, serpentine eye on her small body.

Ten paces. Lilula stopped, crouched, and finished drawing back her arrow. Jadu watched silently, his breath caught in his throat. She was so close to the beast that it could likely reach her in a heartbeat should it choose to. Doubtless its tail could be there in the blink of an eye. Everything relied on that monster not realizing the danger before it.

Just then, as Lilula aimed the arrow for the killing shot, something moved to her left. The maiden did not notice the swift blur, but Jadu saw it from the corner of his eye, and reacted on instinct before fear.

"Lilula! Look out!" He shouted, rushing to intercept the second wyvern.

Lilula released her arrow, hitting the wounded wyvern in the eye and killing it without so much as a dying scream, and then turned to see what Jadu was shouting about.

Chomp. The second, healthy wyvern that had been swooping down from above to devour the Pak maiden, bit down with killing force on Jadu's bow and landed with earthshaking power. The man had thrust Lilula out of the way at the last moment, and reflexively swung his weapon at the approaching danger – fortunately this caused his bow to be the thing caught between the wyvern's teeth and not his arm.

Crunch. The wyvern broke the bow to splinters and then – *snap!* – quickly bit at Jadu's face. The man, however, remembered Lilula's instruction and leapt to the side. *Whip!* The barbed tail lashed out for his chest, but he followed through with his teaching and twisted his body so it passed him by!

Unfortunately, that was the end of his obedience and the beginning of his instincts and reflexes. Although he had been trained to fight demi-humans and humans, not monsters, his habits remained the same; his foe's weapon was before him, and so he grabbed it by the safe spot just below the "blade".

Having missed with its whip, the wyvern tried to pull its tail back, but instead only staggered Jadu, who was holding it in his hand. Angered, the creature roared menacingly before biting once more at the warrior, who, still acting on habit and instinct, leapt out of the way and grasped hold of one of the two large horns on the back of the beast's head, using it as a lever to keep the teeth and snout away from him.

Thus entangled, the two combatants, Jadu the Pak, and the wild northern wyvern, grappled about on the rocky clearing. One moment the wyvern would attempt to pull back its tail or head, trying to free one of its weapons. But whatever distance its sudden tug gave, Jadu forced back with his strength. This was possible only because the wyvern's tail was weak, designed for thrashing not pulling, and its head was leveraged by the man's grasp on its horn.

Sadly, for whatever little the beast could do, Jadu could accomplish just as much. Locked as the two were, all they could do was stagger back and forth across the rough ground, hoping the other would wear out first. It would have been quite comical if not for the extreme peril of the situation.

"Jadu! Watch out for the cliff!" Lilula suddenly cried out in the midst of the battle.

But the maiden's shout came too late, and both Jadu and the wyvern tumbled over the edge, losing their footing and plummeting into open air.

At that moment, Jadu's grip on the wyvern's tail failed him and he grabbed hold of the monster's horn with both hands, hoping fearfully it could still fly despite his added weight. Fortunately, the scaly beast was as capable as its adversary had hoped, and hoisted both itself and Jadu into the air on mighty wings.

The young Pak sighed in understandable relief when the horrible sensation of falling ceased, then just as quickly twisted desperately to evade the thrashing tail of the wyvern. His motion was not enough to escape in the way he had intended, but the sudden shift in weight caused the wyvern's neck to give out to some extent so that its head dropped considerably and rendered Jadu beyond the reach of its whipping weapon.

I pause here briefly to explain the position of things. Lilula is still on the rocky open platform with a dead wyvern some ten paces from her; shot through the eye by her bow. Over the cliff beside her, Jadu and the other wyvern are battling in midair. The wyvern's neck is dropping straight down from its body in a truly painful looking manner because it is not strong enough to lift up Jadu, who is holding onto one of its horns with both hands, and thus twisting its head into an awkward and very uncomfortable position (the beast's neck is perhaps a full man in length). This being the case, its tail is unable to reach Jadu because of his position at the end of its head, which is separated from the tail by the entire length of its body and neck. Ultimately, the only part of the wyvern's body that functions as it wishes at the moment is its wings, which are able to keep the duo from falling and even slowly raise them back towards the platform with extreme strain.

Surprisingly, the madness thus described was only the beginning, for with a manic yelp, Lilula leapt from the side of the cliff and landed on the wyvern's back, where its tail could not reach her. The impact caused the beast to lose height for a moment – jarring everyone involved – before it regained its strength. Unfortunately, with the (however small) added weight of the maiden, the mighty creature was no longer able to rise, but was, in fact, slowly dropping towards the ground.

Whilst laughing, Lilula stretched out her left hand towards the wyvern's matching wing. Roots twirled off of her wrist and formed into a long vine which she lashed out and wrapped around the clawed tip of the flapping limb, some man and a half away from her.

"Jadu!" She shouted to her companion. "When we get near the water, drop in!"

Jadu heard the command and hastily looked around beneath him: the waterfall afore mentioned cascaded down the cliffside and then joined a channel of runoff from higher up the mountain, the combined flows forming a small, swift moving river. What Lilula was speaking of, though, was the water at the base of the fall – it looked deep enough to land in if one were less than ten times his own height above it.

Having already seen these things, Lilula tugged on the vine that connected her hand and the wyvern's wing, causing the beast to swerve to the left and lose height at the same time, diving straight for the river.

"Weeeeeeeeeee!" She cried out in joy as Jadu screamed in terror below.

Splash! Despite Lilula's plan of gently dropping her companion into the pool, both of them and the wyvern wound up submerged in the water… only to come up flailing, thrashing, shouting, and roaring a few seconds later.

Within a moment, though, Lilula had managed to wrap her "vine whip" around the wyvern's maw, sealing shut its fangs and teeth, while still maintaining her position on its back. Jadu, on the other hand, had released the monster's horn and been forced some distance away during the blind underwater struggle. A few cuts had appeared on his torso and limbs, but none of them were severe and he had yet to notice even the worst of the lot.

"Jadu, look" Lilula called out as the wyvern thrashed about at the surface of the water. "I'm a dragon rider!"

Jadu released a short, barking laugh of disbelief at the remark while at the same time struggling to comprehend what he was seeing. His thoughts were cut down just then though as his back collided with a rock, causing him to cry out in pain – the current had caught him, and was pulling him rapidly along the river!

"Jadu! Watch out for the rocks!"

Crack. Jadu's head collided with another large stone as he turned to navigate his path. Shaking off the dizziness and wiping the wet fur out of his eyes, he began to paddle left and right as needed in a desperate attempt to avoid the obstacles in his way and keep himself from being dashed to bits. It was no use; a fallen log lay across the surface of the river and forced the Pak under.

Buried beneath the raging waters, all Jadu could do was thrash and struggle to reach the surface. But no sooner would his snout break free from the aquatic storm and breathe in a gulp of air than he would be forced back under by the furious current. Suddenly, however, just as he began to fear he would soon become exhausted and drown, his hand caught hold of solid, dry purchase above the water's surface.

With a jerk that was not his own, the Pak was on land again – but whatever had pulled him from the river had also begun to drag him along the ground. Wiping the water from his eyes, Jadu looked towards what he had taken hold of: a bull moose's antlers. Likely the regal creature had been trying to drink from the river.

Regardless of the details, the massive animal bucked and reared its head with an angry snort, pulling Jadu from the ground and flinging him to his feet – but there was nothing to land on! The river had flowed strong and fast, and cascaded nearby over a second cliff, forming yet another waterfall. It was over that precipice the moose tried to throw Jadu.

Not so easily disposed of, however, the young Pak caught hold of the rocky ground with his toes and thrust forward his other hand to take grip of the moose's second antler. Thus Jadu found himself suspended over open oblivion with his only lifeline being his toes on the ground and his hands on the crown of the mighty animal before him – if the moose's strength failed for even a moment, both of them would plummet to their death.

But the royal beast's strength faltered not and – for sake of self – it pulled Jadu back onto flat ground, where it immediately began to thrash its head back and forth in an attempt to shake his grip. Jadu, uncertain what else to do, held on, bracing himself as best he could in resistance to the ruthless tossing he was receiving. More than once, yes often, he lost his footing for a moment, but always he regained it quickly.

The moose soon tired of its fruitless attempts though, and lowered its head. Then, with all its incredible might, the wild beast pushed forward, charging Jadu with unstoppable power in a contest of strength! If the young Pak's grip were to fail, or his footing be lost, he would doubtless be trampled! And so, determined not to be slain by some ordinary hoofed beast when he had – somehow – survived grappling with a wyvern, the warrior dug his toes into the earth beneath him and pressed forward with all his own might.

It is with a sigh that I say the moose was stronger, naturally.

Jadu's resistance was short lived; a small trench was dug as his feet slid backwards along the ground, and then his footing failed him. But he had known from the moment he braced himself for that contest he could not win. No Pak could outpower a full-grown moose. Therefore, just before his footing was gone completely, he leapt up from the ground, keeping firm hold of the moose's antlers, wrapped his legs around his adversary's neck and shoulders, and clamped his fangs down around its throat.

Although taken by surprise, the mighty animal trumpeted defiantly as its head drooped from the weight upon it. Jadu only tightened his bite. Thud. The moose dropped to its knees and smashed the Pak against the hard ground. He tightened his bite again.

…Seconds passed until, at last, with a final trumpet sound, the moose surrendered and fell to its side on the soil. Even then, though, Jadu did not loosen his bite; waiting patiently until he could no longer feel the animal's fading breath.

Huff, huff. Huff… huff…… The thunderous breathing stopped, and the regal beast lay still and lifeless. Only then did the warrior Pak finally loose his fangs and creep slowly away.

"Jadu! Look out!"

Jadu stood and turned at the sound of Lilula's voice just in time to see the wyvern from before rushing upon him, the maiden herself being swung to and fro as it thrashed its head back and forth, one of the her vines wrapped around its maw to keep its mouth sealed. Suddenly, the muzzling creeper snapped and Lilula was thrown violently away from the beast, first striking the ground near the other Pak but then tumbling further.

Newly rid of what it likely considered a pest, the wyvern lifted its head and opened its mouth wide, undoing the coil around its jaws with a roar. This done, the scaly giant lowered its terrible gaze upon the two Pak not thirty human paces away – its eyes like coals of hatred and hunger, burning with malice.

Another roar, and a flash of scales! The monster was upon them – bolting forward with savage speed!

Thud. Jadu could not say why, but he had struck the creature a solid blow across the snout using his fist. Perhaps he was simply tired and his mind was slowing down? Truth be told, the last of his fear had burned away against the moose, and his instincts were all that was left to him at that time. He had been trained to fight, and so fight he did.

Now, as one might suppose, the wyvern had not expected such a direct attack, and was temporarily stunned by the blow. But the reprieve granted by this was short, and the beast soon sought revenge. With a growl, the creature stomped forward and swung its head like a club, smashing its skull against Jadu's chest when his reflexes failed him.

Thus, for the second time in that same hour, Jadu felt his footing vanish over the edge of a cliff, and then plummeted towards the earth. This time, however, there was no wyvern to catch him, and no water to soften his landing. The only thing beneath him, far far below, was sharp stones and jagged boulders.

But 'twas not that brave hound's fate to die that day.

Without a moment's hesitation, Lilula dashed across the ground and dove after her companion. As she fell, wooden flesh grew from her back, spreading out into skeletal sails, and upon that oaken frame leaves like feathers began to form. Within seconds, verdant wings of foliage had sprouted from the maiden's back, and propelled her downward.

Passing Jadu by, the winged Pak swooped first down and then back up, rising to meet him. Furthermore, just before the two collided, in which case she would doubtless have been crushed, a torrent of wind rushed out of her, like to when she had faced the Keeper a few days before. The gale slowed Jadu's fall, and added power to her own wings, allowing the small maiden to catch hold of her hefty companion and lift them both higher into the air.

The force faded quickly though, and Lilula knew she could not return the two of them all of the way to the clifftop.

"Jadu, catch the wall." She ordered, releasing the other Pak as she veered towards the cliffside.

Jadu, who had until then been staring at Lilula's wings with his mind shattered into a hundred pieces, regained his focus as he felt her let go of him, and turned to clutch desperately at the wall. The rocks were rough and solid, and his hands and feet easily found grip despite being wet. A moment later, Lilula landed next to him, her wings folded on her back as she also took hold of the cliffside.

"You have wings!" Jadu exclaimed.

"Of course I have-... I... forgot to tell you about my powers, didn't I?" Lilula replied.

"How could you forget to mention something like that!"

The maiden sighed. "Sorry. I'm used to them, so I forget that things like wings are... um..."

"Unusual?" The other Pak suggested, seeing his friend was struggling for words.

"Yeah! What you said! Unusual."

Jadu groaned in disbelief and looked up. Leaving the conversation for later, it appeared they had somewhere between five and six men in height between themselves and the top of the cliff.

"Well, I'm going to go finish off that wyvern." Lilula said, leaping off the wall and catching herself midair with her wings. "Meet me at the top."

Jadu could only watch as the maiden flew off, leaving him alone on the side of a cliff, several stories above certain death below. He was unsure if he should be proud of her confidence in him, or annoyed that she had so quickly abandoned him. Perhaps both? Either way, there was certainly nothing she could do to help him at the moment, and wishing for her to be there was only selfishness. These things decided, he started to climb.

Just then, a roar sounded out like a call to arms and the wyvern came soaring overhead, chasing Lilula into open air with its maw gaping. The maiden swerved and dodged like a frenzied sparrow, evading snaps and chomps from the terrible fangs of the reptilian flyer.

Spinning under her adversary's jaws, the young Pak reached behind her and took hold of her three remaining arrows. Jadu's had long since been washed away by the current of the river, but she had managed to maintain her own.

The wyvern snapped again and Lilula dodged to the side, throwing one of the arrows at its eye like a dart. The creature merely blinked as the projectile bounced harmlessly off of its scaled eyelid, and then growled in anger and spun after its prey. There followed shortly another narrow dodge of the monster's teeth before the second arrow was thrown, also missing its mark.

With only one shaft left, Lilula took to the clouds, rising rapidly through the sky as though aiming to reach the heavens. The wyvern followed like a cat after a mouse, gaining slowly. As the duo rose, the maiden's leafy wings beat quiet and smooth on the air – a gentle breeze – but the wyvern's cracked like thunder with every motion, echoing out as if a broken bell rung to declare the approach of death.

Flap. Flap. Crack. Crack. Flap. Flap. Crack. Crack. Crack. The wyvern closed the last of the distance between it and its prey, opened wide its killing jaws, and clamped down with lethal power. But at the last moment Lilula ceased to fly and instead leaned backwards, rotating through the air like a graceful dancer, with her body arcing perfectly over the wyvern's nose as its teeth closed on emptiness. Such grace turned to brutality the next moment though, as the maiden plummeted beside her foe and brought the arrow plunging deep into its astonished eye with both hands.

Surprised and wounded, the creature flailed and roared in agony while Lilula flapped backwards and away to avoid the thrashing tail, talons, and fangs. No good; a few seconds later the monster turned its remaining eye on the one who had harmed it, rage like never before burning behind its iris.

With a feral cry of vengeance, fire erupted from the open maw of the wyvern, flaring towards Lilula. The maiden answered in kind, thrusting both her hands forward and releasing a bolt of lightning from her palms, bones flashing white through her flesh and fur. The two elements of destruction collided in a contest of raging power, in which the fire was dispersed by the thunderclap, and a blue bolt struck the wyvern, scorching its scales black.

Struck yet another blow, the mighty creature flapped its wings hard, trying to stay in the air – but its strength waned quickly and it began to plummet, passing Jadu and falling to the earth below like a heavy stone. Meanwhile, as the monster vanished beneath her line of sight, Lilula's arms drooped to her sides and she bowed her head, breathing heavily while she wearily drifted towards the plateau beneath her.

Crack. Crack. Crack! Opening her eyes at the noise, the maiden looked down. The wyvern was rushing up towards her, its one remaining eye open wide, bloodshot, and seeping out endless waves of murderous intent. Though battered and scorched, the monster had not yet surrendered or died, and was hellbent on slaying the winged Pak above it.

Now, Jadu, still clinging to the cliff, saw the beast rising in rapid ascent from below him, beheld the fury in its eye, and heard its wrathful cry. *All-King preserve us!* He thought, surprised, although not at the wyvern's resilience. *That beast is me!*

Indeed, it was the truth. Had he not had that same fire in his eyes when he attacked the Blackhounds? Had he not released a similar cry in his madness to slay them? Had he not also endured terrible hurts simply to satiate his anger? The wyvern before him was a monster, so such fury was only natural. But had *he* truly fallen so far in his rage? Had he truly degraded himself into such a beast? Abandoning all reason, all logic, all good things, and harboring nothing but bitterness and vengeance?

That is in the past. Jadu declared within his very soul. *I will resist that madness with all I am.*

His own moral standing decided, the young Pak then turned to face the problem of the wyvern, and Lilula's imminent peril. If he had been struck down despite his rage, surely that beast could be as well. So, out of time and desperate, Jadu tore a loose stone from the side of the cliff he clung to, turned to aim, and cast it with all his strength at the murderous winged predator.

The attack was a stray arrow. A one in a hundred chance. The odds of rain without clouds or a storm without wind. But miracles do occur from time to time, and this just happened to be one of them. The stone, as though guided by heaven, struck the wyvern's remaining eye, blinding it with a horrific shriek.

A moment later, Lilula swerved out of the way of the maddened, sightless monster and swung weakly towards the cliff face, catching herself against it heavily. Jadu, in turn, glanced in her direction to ensure she was safe, and then looked back towards their adversary.

The wyvern was flapping about in the air madly, breathing fire and thrashing its tail at invisible foes until, frenzied and senseless, it flew towards the cliff. At that moment, Jadu's eyes shot wide – the beast was flying straight towards him!

Turning back to the mountain wall, the Pak pulled himself tight against the stones, closed his eyes, and held on with all his might. A second later, the whole cliffside was shaken as the wyvern crashed into it, still clawing and snapping wildly.

Sensing his enemy's presence, Jadu opened his eyes and turned his head, but only to find the wyvern's face was directly beside his own.

In reflex and panic, the man caught hold of the back of the weakened creature's head and smashed its chin against the rocks. Now the beast was *not at all* approving of such a thing, howled in anger, and tried to turn and snap at its attacker. Jadu smashed its head against the wall again. Again it roared and tried to turn. Once more he smashed it. Again and again – Three more times he battered that wyvern's skull against the rocks, unable to think of any better strategy nor able anymore to be afraid. As afore said, his fear was long since burned up.

At last, enraged with such treatment, the wyvern roared yet again and then freed its head with a mighty wrench before clawing its way up the mountain side. Now, Jadu, not wanting to be crushed as the beast climbed past him, swung out of the way on one foot, clinging to the mountain with a single hand as well. A few moments later, though, the wyvern vanished over the top of the cliff.

The young Pak regained his grip, and turned to face Lilula.

"You can shoot lightning from your hands!" He exclaimed.

"You just beat a wyvern's skull against the side of a cliff." She replied. "I'd say we're even."

Jadu snorted but did not respond while, to his left, Lilula's wings decayed as though rotting branches and fell from her shoulders. After this, it took only a momentary reprieve before the maiden had caught her breath and started to look upwards.

"Let's go." She finally said, beginning to climb.

To her right, Jadu silently accepted the decision and followed her example, making his own way up the rocky cliff face. As could be expected, when the two reached the top a short time later, they were greeted with the sight of the blinded wyvern raging about in madness on the open ground some threescore paces away.

The area around the river that had drug Jadu along was a wide plateau of rocks and soil intermixed, perhaps two hundred paces from cliff to waterfall, and of unknown width. It was on this large platform that the two Pak and the mad creature then stood.

"Did you kill that moose?" Lilula asked, pointing at the corpse off to their side.

Jadu glanced at the body and then replied.

"Yes."

"With what?"

"My teeth."

There was a considerable pause after the simple answer.

"Impressive." Lilula finally said.

Jadu nodded. "Thank you."

"Well then," The maiden continued, turning from the dead moose and towards the whirlwind of claws and fire that was the wyvern. "would you like to finish off our prey this afternoon."

"If I have any say at all, I will not so much as go near that beast." Jadu replied emphatically. "Slay it with your lightning."

Lilula smiled. "Okay."

With that, the maiden lifted her arms up beside her, light cackling around them, and then thrust them forward, sending out a devastating blast of power. As for Jadu, he could only watch in awe as the lightning arced out of his companion's body and into the wyvern. And as for the wyvern, well, it roared its final defiance before collapsing to the ground after a few seconds of constant duress, smoking and blackened.

In the aftermath, Lilula let her arms drop to her sides as the lightning stopped, and stood staring at the fallen predator. Jadu gazed upon the beast as well. Just then though, without warning, Lilula collapsed to her hands and knees, a strange noise coming out of her mouth.

Seeing this, Jadu started and rushed to her side, putting his hands on the maiden's shoulders and shaking her gently.

"Lilula!" He called. "Lilu, are you alright?"

There was no answer, but the strange noise continued. After a moment, Jadu realized what it was.

"Are you laughing?" He asked seriously.

Lilula, truth be told, most certainly was. Moreover, she continued to laugh in response to the austere query, tears of mirth flowing down her nose and dripping to the ground.

"We almost died!" She exclaimed.

"Which is why you should not be laughing!" Jadu replied.

"But we didn't!" Lilula continued. "And everything went so badly too! Haha! That was ridiculous!"

Jadu shook his head in confusion and then shook Lilula to try and break whatever spell she was under.

"Stop this madness at once." He commanded. "We were nearly killed."

The maiden sat up on her haunches, causing Jadu to wrongly believe she was obeying him, and then dove into his chest with a violent embrace.

"We'll have plenty of times to cry later, Jadu." She said, calming her mirth only enough to speak somewhat seriously. "But that was fun. Why take the joy from something that doesn't deserve mourning?"

Huh?

Jadu's eyes opened wide as the words sunk into him. Meanwhile Lilula continued to chuckle, her laughter muffling itself in his tunic. *She speaks true.* The young man thought. *No tragedy has befallen us and we are unscathed. I should be grateful, not irked. But still… why does she laugh?*

"Lilula," Jadu said. "I see the wisdom in your words. But why laugh now? I see nothing humorous."

Lilula pulled her face out of Jadu's chest and looked up at him.

"You punched a wyvern in the nose." She answered, trying to contain herself. "You smashed a wyvern's head against the wall. You killed a moose with your bare hands! You fell off of *two* cliffs in less time than it takes to eat a meal! YOU WRESTLED A TINY DRAGON!"

The exuberant maiden finally lost control once more and fell to the ground, rolling around and laughing madly with her hands clasped over her chest. Jadu only stared at her in uncertainty… at first. But the laughter was contagious, and the moment he imagined what the battle just past must have looked like from her view, a hoarse bark escaped his mouth. The image was ridiculous. After all, the wyvern was at least four times his size, with fangs as long as daggers and enough strength to crush him with ease. What sort of madman would grapple with such a beast?

Faced with such an impossible picture, there was only one response: Jadu also broke out into waves of laughter.

…

When at last the two Pak regained their faculties, they promptly got to work; The wyvern and moose were both skinned and field dressed (the former being much trickier because of its monstrous size), the skins were weighted to the bottom of the stream to be cleaned, and the meat was started smoking over a large fire made from an abundance of dead branches found in the area. The duo also took special care to burn origun root in the blaze so as to ward off any other wyverns in the area – the beasts find the smell atrocious. By the time all this was done, the night had long since come, and the moon was nearing its apex.

"You realize we cannot carry an entire wyvern *and* an entire moose worth of meat, do you not?" Jadu asked as he and Lilula sat around the dying fire, staring into the embers.

"Once it's smoked I have ways to preserve it." The maiden answered. "Anything we aren't going to bring with I'll get ready tomorrow morning and then hide it. I have stashes like that all around the forest, this will just be another one."

Jadu nodded. He had not a clue how his companion could protect so much meat from rot and beast with so little preparation, but she had no reason to lie and he had no reason to doubt her, so he believed it without a word.

"The hides should be cleaned off by the morning as well." Lilula continued. "I'll make two backpacks out of the moose, it should only take me an hour since they don't need to be very good, and I can always improve them during later nights."

Jadu nodded again, still staring into the coals of the fire.

"Lilula," He asked after a short pause. "where did you get those powers? Your wings, those vines, the lightning, and that control you had over the wind?"

The maiden sighed and leaned herself back, staring up at the stars and tapping her chin as she thought of an answer.

"Do you know much about Silvertongue?" She inquired at last.

"Only a little." Jadu replied. "I know that Silvertongues use powerful words from the Ancient Language, along with certain, usually rare, objects in order to manipulate the world around them to their will."

"Yes, well, it's similar." Lilula explained. "Only *I* am the item, and I don't need to speak any commands."

Jadu turned his eyes to the maiden. "My apologies, but I do not understand."

The gray-furred dog bit her lip and thought of a better way to explain it.

"You know how when two people are really close, how they know what the other one wants without ever needing to say anything." She began. "Well, it's like that with me and the elements. I've been with them so long, that I can just think of something I want them to do for me, and they do it. Or… certain things, at least. I don't need an item or a command, just a wish."

Jadu nodded slowly. "I believe I understand."

"I'm not sure how it works." Lilula continued. "I think it has something to do with the 'Astral Body' that Silvertongues talk about. Mama said my Astral Body has become linked to the elemental 'Astral Body' and I now draw strength from it. But I'm not sure what she means by those things."

"That is fine." Her companion said plainly. "The way you explained it as being like a close friend made enough sense for me. I am no Silvertongue nor a scholar. Simple explanations such as that suit me perfectly."

Lilula beamed and then turned back to the fire as Jadu did the same. Presently, the maiden chuckled.

"What is it?" Jadu asked.

"I was just thinking again on everything that happened today." She answered. "It was fun. We should do it again sometime."

Jadu chuckled as well. "Perhaps."

"You don't sound very excited?"

"I do not relish the thought of being killed any more now than I did this morning." The big Pak answered. "We were lucky this time, I doubt it will be the same in the future."

Lilula smiled. "What luck?" She asked, her voice full of mirth. "We earned that victory on strength and skill. You of all people should know that; you fought toe to toe with a wyvern! How many times do I need to say it before you understand how amazing that was?"

Jadu snorted humorously. "I only bumbled around in an attempt to survive." He replied. "You were far more graceful, beautiful even."

"Don't jest." Lilula replied with a wave of her hand and openly fake embarrassment.

"I do not." Jadu insisted. "When you fought against that wyvern with your wings, you were like some mad angel of legend – controlling the winds and wielding thunder in your hands."

This time the maiden laughed. "So I'm a beautiful thunder wielding angel and you're a beastly strong warrior?" She asked, although it was spoken more as a statement.

Jadu smiled and laughed as well. "Yes, well, I suppose we both have our strengths. Although I feel mine are lesser than yours after this."

With the fire burned to mere coals and nothing more to say, Lilula rolled her eyes and then lay her tired body down. The other Pak noticed his companion's actions and copied her, resting his head on a stone.

"I suppose we had best get some sleep." He said, closing his eyes wearily. "I will see you in the morning."

…

…

…

"Jadu…"

Jadu opened his eyes and looked towards Lilula – the maiden was sitting upright.

"Yes?" He asked.

"…It's going to be cold tonight on this plateau… Could… we sleep beside each other?"

"…Of course."

With the consent spoken, Lilula crawled across the stones and lay down beside her companion, curling up with her cheek against his chest. Know that such a thing is not strange or sensual for Pak, it is only a sign of trust and affection – a mark of friendship.

"Thank you, you Mighty Hound." The maiden whispered with a laugh behind her voice.

Jadu closed his arms around her with a faint smile and then whispered his reply.

"Of course, Thunder Angel."

…

Thus comforted in one another's embrace, the two friends drifted off into a peaceful sleep. The journey ahead of them would be long and treacherous, full of tears and trials just as Lilula had predicted. But for that time, they were happy and at rest. A calm before a terrible storm…

The Serpent's Heir. Venom of the Great Snake flowing through his veins. Jadu was more than he realized, and a great weight that he was unaware of rested on his shoulders.

And what of the mysterious Mother Garnage? What was her role in all of it?

What of the other "Keepers"? What of the Blackhounds? What of Jadu's pack, betrayed by Red Maw?

Yes, a storm was approaching, filled with many tragedies and threats. A storm, whirling about with mad power and unlimited carnage. A storm, coming to destroy and to harm. But what are heroes made for, if not to brave such a storm? And what is the point of a tale if not to follow such heroes… straight to the eye of the vortex!

The Siege of Castle Walsin
- a tale of Torric, The Fist

Clang. Clang. Clang. The sound of metal striking metal was quiet, yet it was enough to wake the curious villager. Surely the blacksmith was not up so early? Leaving his bed and his sleeping – and also very pregnant – wife, the young man opened the door to find that it was still the dead of night.

Walking to the back room, the villager saw that the third inhabitant of the house was not in his bed either, nor in the room at all. That could mean only one thing.

Wrapping a fur cloak around himself to fend off the night air, the man quietly exited his home and headed towards the sound of striking metal. It was dark, and a single lamp lit the outside world, shining from within the blacksmith's workshop. Towards that light the man walked, already knowing what he would find.

Torric, many years after the battle soon to be retold, no longer known as "The Fist" but rather titled "Knight of Heaven", was carefully mending his armor in the midnight watch, the lamp burning on the worktable beside him. The villager, William, approached and stood beside the knight.

"It is late, Torric." He said. "Should you not be resting?"

Torric lowered the hammer in his hand and turned to his friend.

"I must be ready, no matter what." He said simply, his voice carrying no malice or impatience, only truth. "You saw the battle earlier today. There is no telling when danger may come. My diligence and my duty is to be ever ready with the weapons the All-King has granted me."

With that, the knight turned back to his armor and continued to quietly mend it.

"I am sorry to have woken you." He said sincerely to his friend.

William, however, did not respond – his eyes were fixed on the bandages across Torric's back, neck, and arms. The knight wore no shirt, so they were easy to see. He had been wounded, not terribly, but enough to doubtless cause considerable pain. The battle he had fought earlier that day to protect that tiny nameless village, a battle against three powerful Zrell Accusers, was something most men would have failed to win. He was not unscathed as it was.

But it was not Torric's diligence despite the pain, nor his tolerance of his injuries, nor his devout loyalty that kept William silent at that time. No. It was the endless crisscrossing scars on the knight's back and limbs; Shadows of a hundred and more wounds of diverse kinds, all fierce enough to leave a permanent mark that he could clearly see even then. What hells had that knight faced? What horrors had he seen?

"Torric," William began timidly. "I know you dislike speaking of your past, but… have you fought Zrell before?"

Torric did not stop working as he answered. "I have."

"Are any of these scars…?"

The knight nodded. "Some."

William swallowed and fell silent. A long time passed in that quiet atmosphere, but eventually the villager turned and left, returning to his home and his wife, Tarya.

With the young man's departure, Torric was left alone in the light of his lamp, working as quietly as he could on his battered armor that the blacksmith had been kind enough to lend him the supplies needful to repair. He was tired. But he had been much more tired many times before. Moreover, he had meant what he said. He felt it was his duty to be ready whenever a new threat might arrive, to protect those around him at any cost. That was what his loyalty to his king – the All-King – deserved. Nothing less.

But it would have been a lie to say he was perfectly focused at that time. A man such as him has many memories and nightmares to avoid, and one such phantom was clawing at his mind even then. The battle with the Zrell had awoken it.

It is that memory, that story, that is here retold.

…

Over twenty years before Torric's midnight conversation with William, the brave knight was but a simple soldier.

Now, before I go further, I must explain some things. The nation of Valtara, Torric's home, is divided into a number of "kingdoms", each one ruled by a king. A High King reigns over the united kingdoms, ensuring they remain unified and loyal to the Supreme Scroll – a remarkable document of brilliance and great importance which can be discussed in detail somewhere else.

However, just before the time of this story about Torric the soldier, the northern kingdom of Kasil rebelled against the rest of Valtara, refusing to uphold the statutes demanded by the Supreme Scroll. The High King – not wanting to send the united army and further increase Kasil's claim to independence, and thus also the risk of other nations choosing to involve themselves – ordered Kasil's neighboring kingdom, Oser, to handle the problem, and sent them funds.

It was just after this civil war began that Torric joined the Oser military. And 'twas fortunate timing for him too, for when he joined, recruits such as himself were trained a full month before being sent to battle, rather than simply being armed and marched off to die as would all too soon become the custom.

Now, the river Agar forms the border of Oser and Kasil, and there was at that time only one bridge across the river that had not yet been destroyed in the war: the drawbridge of the castle of Duke Walsin of Oser. As a note, Duke Walsin was a cowardly, boastful man who remained near the battle only for the sake of his fame. His castle, unfortunately for him though, was a strategic centerpiece, and the side that controlled it controlled also a powerful natural barrier.

After nearly a year of fighting, Kasil forces had driven out Oser occupation and held near total control of their homeland. The last obstacle between them and a sovereign fortification would be to control Castle Walsin and its drawbridge.

There was more danger here for Oser than simply losing a war, however. You see, Oser was drained of men and gold, as well as morale. Kasil, on the other hand, continued to receive mercenary reinforcements hired by their seemingly endless treasury. Where those mysterious funds came from is a different story.

Therefore, if Kasil were to claim Castle Walsin, there was no guarantee they would stop there. The odds were high they would press farther into Oser territory, pillage the surrounding land, and perhaps even claim it as their own. At that point, the High King would have no choice but to declare full out war, and thus potentially spark the participation of another nation.

So then, we see that at that time, the war, and potentially all of Valtara, rested on the control of Castle Walsin. Moreover, as you may have guessed, Torric was stationed at that fateful outpost; a young man, not yet more than twenty years of age, with a month of training, and less than a handful of other battles under his belt. He was certainly no hero at that time. No legend. No knight. He was just another soldier, waiting for either reinforcements, or the inevitable assault. And that soldier awoke one dreadful night to the sound of blood curdling shrieks and the screams of dying men.

Hastened by the shouting of their captain and the terrible tumult outside, Torric and his squad leapt from their cots and equipped themselves quickly. Boots were tied, tunics thrown on with chainmail shirts over them, belts buckled, swords grabbed, and shields fastened in a matter of seconds. These were their arms; simple weapons and armor to give them the barest of fighting chances.

Thus equipped, the squad of ten and their captain at last emerged from their tent and into utter darkness. The clouds were thick overhead, blocking out the starlight and the moon. The courtyard could not be seen around them, nor the walls of the castle. All was dark save the piddly light coming from their own tent door. Where were the torches? Where were the night watchmen?

A scream caught the attention of the bewildered soldiers, and they turned towards the sound. Already though the cry had been replaced with a noisy crunching. And if that t'were not enough to shake a man, then the multitude of other screams and roars all about within the tar-black courtyard was.

"Monsters in the walls!" Someone shouted in the distance.

"Someone help!"

"Run!"

"Get torches!"

"Where are the blasted lights!"

Torric and his group of fellow soldiers stood uncertainly outside of their tent door, weapons at the ready. They could see next to nothing. How were they to act?

"Sir," One of the soldiers began to say timidly.

"Speak boy." The captain replied.

"I hear the drawbridge."

At the word, all of the soldiers stopped breathing for a moment and listened... The lad was right. The unmistakable creak of the drawbridge lowering was flowing through the courtyard, nigh drowned beneath the shouts and shrieking.

"What in the Pit is happening?" The captain swore. "Is this the attack? ...All right then, ere's are plan. First-"

The soldier never finished, for a massive form appeared out of the darkness and ended his life with one swipe of its claws.

"Monster!" Someone cried.

"Kill it!" Another shouted.

Already two more soldiers had been cast aside like rags by the hulking shadow, yet Torric rushed in all the same. The man swung his sword at the beast, but it came short in the darkness! As though in retribution, a heavy weight struck him across the shield, ripping the wooden barrier to shreds, cutting his arm, and toppling him onto his back.

In those few moments since the fight began, one of the soldiers had rushed back into the tent and retrieved a lamp. Reemerging just then, the blessed light fell on the assailer – a Zrell.

A full head and shoulders taller than any of them, the scaled behemoth towered over the soldiers. Her skull was curved and long, like a giant beak filled with knifelike teeth. Her tail thrashed behind her with deathly power and strength, and her claws glistened in the lamplight like twinkling stars of ill-omen.

"Zrell!" One of Torric's comrades tried to scream, but the word remained eternally in his gashed throat as he crumpled and fell lifeless to the ground.

Undeterred, Torric himself rolled over and stood back up as the monstrous demi-human assailed his companions. With a shout, the young man swung his sword at her back – but it glanced off, leaving only a thin cut. The Zrell had felt the strike though, and spun around, swinging her killing claws at his head. The soldier managed to parry the attack with his blade, but it cost him his balance – he would not be able to withstand a second blow! Just then, however, a sword tip pierced through the darkdweller's chest from behind, causing her to release a blood chilling cry of agony.

The blade disappeared a moment later, pulled out of the Zrell, but then reappeared at a different place, earning another deafening shriek.

"Die Pit-fiend!" The burly, half-Ursa soldier behind her roared, stabbing the giant through the chest once more.

With the third blow the Zrell finally died and fell to the ground.

…After a short pause, Torric looked up from the slain beast, towards his comrade, and then nodded his appreciation. But no sooner had he done this than the hideous head of a second Zrell appeared out of the darkness, caught the burly halfblood by the arm, and drug him screaming into the shadows.

"Dragon scat!" One of the other soldiers swore, leaping towards the man who held the lamp as though the light offered safety.

Torric, for his part, stared at the open air that had moments before been a friend, and then stepped into the lamplight as well, ignoring the sound of crunching bones that came from less than twenty paces away.

"Thank the All-King, more light." Someone in the distance said.

Looking up, Torric saw that the main doors to the castle had been opened partially, and a detachment of troops was emerging with torches. Thud. The joy was short-lived, for that very second the sound of the drawbridge striking the ground was heard, and with it, a distant warcry, and the neighing of horses.

"To the gate!" The newly arriving soldiers shouted. "To the gate! All soldiers to the gate!"

"No way in the Pit." The man behind Torric exclaimed. "We'll be ripped apart from behind."

"Assuming we make it there." Another added.

"Stop crying and act like men!" Torric snapped at his comrades, striking one of them in the gut angrily. "You're soldiers, act like it!"

Without waiting for a response, the young warrior turned and rushed after the torchbearers as he had been ordered. If he was commanded to protect the gate, by gods or by none, that is what he would do!

As he ran through the darkness, a murderous roar sounded off to his side, and Torric dove for the ground, evading the certain demise of the Zrell's claws by only a hairbreadth. Rolling back to his feet, the young man spun around slashing, uncertain where his foe would be. His sword was caught in the titan's iron grip and torn from his hand.

His victory decided, the scaled savage roared at Torric and showed all of his many teeth in the darkness; it seemed he was gloating. Such smugness made Torric angry. So angry, in fact, that – *crack!* – he struck the ugly giant's snout with enough force to break his own hand. That, in turn, enraged the Zrell, who retaliated by delivering a similar, although clawed, blow to Torric's chest.

The warrior was thrown backwards onto the ground, pain searing across his slashed upper body as his torn tunic turned crimson, the chainmail over it cut through like parchment. The Zrell roared out in a gloating manner again, and then fell dead – beheaded by one of the other soldiers.

"Get up. We need every man fighting." Someone said, helping Torric to his feet.

The wounded soldier staggered to a stand, retrieved his sword, and then followed after his savior. Not far away he could see the gate, illuminated by many torches. But the men defending the opening were suddenly dashed apart by a rushing tide of horsemen, cut down in an inescapable flood of hooves and iron.

"Pit-fiend." The man leading Torric cursed, stopping in his tracks.

Seeing this, Torric stopped as well, panting. His mind was fading away quickly, his reason and logic seeping out. Danger was as abstract to him as mathematics, and strategy as far-fetched as gods that actually cared.

"Retreat!" Someone shouted. "Make for the doors!"

The soldier beside Torric turned at the command and headed for the entrance to the castle itself, their orders changing for the second time in only seconds.

"This is madness!" The man exclaimed.

Meanwhile, Torric was forced to take deep, painful breaths to fight off his growing sense of fatigue while he followed as quickly as he could. By the time they arrived, the castle doors had been fully opened. Now, these doors were at least three men in height, and eight men – shoulder to shoulder – in total width, far larger than they should be for a castle of that size. But the duke, as aforementioned, was a proud man and demanded the gaudiest entranceway he could have. Thus: the indefensible doors Torric and his fellow soldiers now fled towards.

Before the open doorway, out of which shone much light, stood a row of archers, firing upon the enemy cavalry while a scattered defense of men armed with sword and shield stood in a half circle before them, warding off any foes who came too close. The invading horsemen, for their part, all held torches in one hand and a sword in the other, and were rushing to and fro across the open courtyard, slaughtering any soldiers who had not yet regrouped with their allies.

Looking across the expanse of the open field, Torric counted four dead Zrell, one live one, and at least a score of his fallen companions.

Those numbers bode ill. The castle's entire defense had been less than threescore as of the night before, and now near half of that number lay dead on the battlefield before the battle had even properly begun. Not to mention their foes were already past the gates.

Turning away from the carnage, Torric reached the row of archers and tried to enter the castle.

"Woah there." A captain – identifiable by his blue sash – said, putting out a forbidding hand. "Get into defensive formation soldier. We need every swordsman we got."

Torric sputtered and froze. "I… need… a healer." He croaked, barely able to put the words together with his fading conscience.

The captain shook his head. "If you can speak you can fight."

Torric swallowed his own bile and blood and turned around, taking his sword in hand and stepping out towards the scattered ring of defenders. It appeared the horsemen had retreated – praise heaven – but now an army of foot-soldiers was rushing across the open drawbridge.

Forget about that.

How long had it been since he had been awoken by the sounds of screaming? Torric wondered. Five minutes? Less? Too much had happened and too fast. There had been too little time to think and no time to mourn. He could not even remember the names of his friends and comrades who now lay dead – his heart numbed by the brutality of the assault.

He could not remember their names, no, but he could remember their faces. Eyes, looks, frowns, smiles – Torric was good with faces. And as he thought about the faces of his dead comrades, a familiar smile came into his mind… A smile with canines that were a tad too long, and teeth a tad too small. A smile that had at one time banished all sadness and fear from him, and melted his heart so he thought it could never become hard again.

That smile had been taken away from him. Torn away by the cruel grasp of death.

That made him angry. Not a new anger. Not a new rage. But an old one. An anger and a bitterness that had given him strength through many hardships and trials, and at that time burned in him once again. And now, carved around his flaming heart that was beating like a hammer in his chest, the deep wounds the Zrell's claws had left on Torric no longer hurt – they only fueled his ire.

Red.

The charging mass of mercenaries and Kasil soldiers arrived, rushing into Torric and his fellow defenders as they tightened their formation. Fearless, the young man met them with a shout of rage.

…

Torric, the Knight of Heaven, set down the blacksmith hammer with a heavy thud and leaned on both his hands wearily. The night was still dark, and he was still alone. His energy had by no means failed him, but his heart was heavy. Somewhere on his chest, lost amongst their late arriving brethren, the old scars from that Zrell ached and burned.

The smile that had given him strength during that battle kept appearing in his mind, unable to be driven out. Even then, so many years later, that age-old anger threatened to consume him. That bitterness and hatred of all things reared its ugly head once more and bared its teeth, begging to devour him.

Therefore, the knight began to weep, tears running in waves from his one good eye as he sobbed quietly into the darkness. He would not surrender to his rage. Some wrath is righteous, but he knew his was not. His anger was only a means of numbing his pain – a liquor to banish his grief. It was so tempting to give in, but he knew it was wrong.

So instead of be bitter, he wept. He wept for the person to whom that smile and a pair of soft green eyes had belonged. He wept for all his mistakes and the many times he had crushed himself only to hide his own pain. All his errors and all his wrongs were poured out once more in those tears.

But as he wept thus, he could feel warm arms wrap around him. No one was there, not in body at least. But the All-King was always with him. And like the Father He was, He would not allow His son to bear even the slightest grief alone.

…

The first wave of an army is always the weakest. Untrained recruits, conscripts, and the cheapest mercenaries are put in the front to wear down the defenders and kill themselves on any immediate threats. The Kasil army assaulting Castle Walsin was no different, and Torric made easy work of the inexperienced soldiers who initially came into his path. He was no klutz with a sword; indeed, he was one of the best swordsmen in his regiment, and his rage gave added strength and passion to his arm.

"The doors!" One of his fellow soldiers cried out in dismay.

"I don't want to die!" Another shouted.

"They can't leave us here!"

"Wait!"

"Fiends! Go to the Pit!"

Torric, heedless to his allies' bitter cries, took a step back to evade an opponent's blade and felt his heel come across something solid. In the midst of the fight, the castle doors had been closed behind him and his comrades.

Now, such a heartless action only made sense from a strategic point of view. The *doors*, although hinged to open either direction, had been opened inward, and thus could only be closed if no invaders were past the *doorframe*. The only way to close them, then, under such a massive assault, was if a group of soldiers were to remain outside and repel the enemy for long enough. Naturally, those sacrificed for this tactical maneuver were not warned of their fate, and only learned of it *after* they were cut off from escape.

And so, amongst those doomed warriors was Torric… who did not care.

Aye, giving no heed to such things as retreat or betrayal whatsoever, the young soldier fought on. Now, through the mass of faces, helmets, and blades, he could see a red Draco – a mercenary of the dragon-kin, covered in blood-red scales, with fire snorting out of his nostrils in angry puffs. At that moment, the moment he beheld him, the courtyard and the battlefield vanished to Torric.

Yes, the young man was no longer in a castle, but standing on a snowy mountaintop with a village of burning houses around him. A great red beast of scales and claws, a dragon, towered in the middle of the burning town, raining fire on the dwellings and inhabitants. Torric was young, not even nine years old. He was reaching out his hand for his parents… who were being enveloped in killing flame.

Slash. Slash. Another invader fell dead to Torric's blade, blood staining his sword and his vision. Red. It was like the dragon. Red. It was like the fire. Slash. Slash. His hand was closer to those of his parents. Slash. Slash. As the battle raged on, more and more red appeared, and his hand got closer and closer. So close. Slash. Slash.

He could almost touch their fingertips! Just a few more blows and their nails would meet! Slash. Slash. Almost there. It was too close. Maybe this time he could reach them! Maybe this time he could finally grasp hold of them!

Infuriated by how near he was to taking hold of his parents's hands once more, Torric released a shout and poured more strength into his attacks. The eyes of his ally soldiers widened as they heard the scream. Torric was unaware of them, but they, at that moment, became aware of him – a madman amongst them, fighting with fury and fire, driving down foe after foe without ever slowing. Encouraged by the maddened warrior, the doomed soldiers of Oser released a battle cry of their own and pressed their defense, valiantly driving away their fear.

Torric was still on that snowy mountaintop though, reaching desperately for hands he could never hold. Red. Red. Red. Blood. Scales. Fire. If only he could reach them. If only he could stretch that final hairbreadth! Their hands were outstretched, and so was his. How could their fingers not touch? How could they not feel one another? Red. Red. Red. He was so close, and the maddening color was all he could see. Blood. Scales. Fire.

…

Torric wiped the tears away and resumed the tedious work of mending his armor. His hand had changed so much since that tragic day, long, long ago. It was no longer the soft, innocent hand of a child, but the calloused hand of a warrior, smeared with the invisible stain of blood, and pale from its constant time beneath armor.

His parents… were long gone. Slain by a dragon when he was but a boy.

The girl to whom that smile and a pair of soft green eyes had belonged, his adopted sister from the orphanage… was also gone. Killed by disease.

He alone was left. He had no family. For a long time he had no friends. And for even longer, he had no hope.

But those times were passed.

Wiping the tears away once more, the Knight of Heaven let his age-old memories turn to scars, just like the wounds from that distant battle had – no longer to be a burden, but a reminder of all he had been carried through.

…

The red before Torric's eyes vanished to the sight of the castle's Silvertongue, Hur. The doors had been opened the slightest bit, and the remaining defenders had been pulled back inside before the passageway was slammed once more and barred with a heavy wooden beam. Therefore, no longer fighting, the young warrior sputtered and blinked while the sanguine color faded from his vision. With the color went some of his fury, and with his fury, his strength.

With a heavy crash, Torric fell to the stone floor of the castle interior, his sight blurring and all of his vigor leaving him. But before he could perish or faint, Hur rolled him onto his back and whispered some strange words before pouring a few drops of liquid onto his chest. The fluid was cold and shocked the young man back awake with such violence that he punched the healer in reflex.

Hur staggered sideways from the blow and then stood back up, rubbing his jaw.

"He'll live." He informed a captain who stood nearby.

Torric grunted in pain and stood up as well, his wounds sealed but tender.

"Good." The captain replied. "We need every sword we have."

Torric could tell by the voice it was the same captain who had forbid him from being healed before, and was assailed with an urge to strike him. He resisted, barely, glared at the captain instead, and then turned to look around.

The castle entryway where he then stood was a tall and wide stone room, roughly square, with a staircase on either side, a hallway in the middle of the back wall, the doors on the front, tapestries hanging all around, and torches lit wherever there was room to spare. Regarding the occupants, there appeared to be Torric, just over a dozen other soldiers, the captain, the Silvertongue Hur, and a man Torric recognized all too well as Duke Walsin's eldest son, the bastard Hark.

"What's the noble brat doing here?" Torric asked one of the other soldiers, whispering into his ear to avoid being overheard.

"The Duke's already fled." The other soldier replied. "He left his kid to command things here. Lucky thing too, he's the one who ordered the doors to be opened, otherwise you and the rest with you would be dead by now."

Torric spit on the ground. "He'll still get no respect from me."

"Heir Hark, what are our orders?" The captain asked, turning to the noble, along with the rest of the soldiers.

This Hark was twenty-one years old, of average height, with medium brown skin (a rare thing in the north), white hair despite his youth, and a single, pitch-black, curved horn on the right side of his head. He was a known illegitimate child of the duke, but his mother's identity was unknown. All that could be safely guessed at was her race – Diabli, the demon-like inhabitants of the Black Spire.

"We have to protect the castle." The noble said, his voice grim. "My father has already fled- Forgive my rudeness… He has left to gather aid, taking a large portion of the troops with him."

"Blasted coward." One of the soldiers muttered quietly beneath his breath.

"I am afraid those you see around you are all of us that remain." Hark continued, ignoring the hushed murmurs of the men. "I know the future looks bleak, but trust me when I say I will fight with you – whatever the outcome."

"What hope is that?" One of the soldiers finally blurted out. "You're just a noble, not even a trained soldier."

"Yeah!" Another agreed.

Hark sighed and bowed his head. "I am no soldier, 'tis true." He said, looking towards the sword at his belt and the iron shield on his arm. "I have faced combat but once, and have little experience, although I do have training."

Suddenly, the noble turned towards the captain. "Captain, you are in charge. I rescind my command. Until the battle ends, consider me but another man."

The captain staggered back, along with some of the other soldiers.

"But Heir Hark, you're the duke's son!" The officer argued.

"That does not matter." Hark replied. "I have no experience and am no strategist. You are better suited for the roll of militant leader."

The captain did not immediately respond, looking instead as though he were struggling for words. Just then, however, a heavy blow sounded against the thick wooden doors – a battering ram!

Now, you should know that Castle Walsin was designed, aside from the gaudy doors, to be resistant to siege. The drawbridge to cross the river required several men to hoist, and opened into a large walled courtyard. Against the back of that courtyard was the castle proper, in which Torric and his comrades then hid. The castle proper itself was multiple stories, possessed towers, turrets, archer holes, and many rooms, as well as a dungeon and armory.

Opposite to the drawbridge courtyard, through the main castle, was a smaller walled courtyard with a portcullis leading into the open country. Effectively, if invaders entered from either side, they would control but one courtyard, and thus one gate, and could not control the other without also controlling the castle interior between.

Unfortunately, despite these defensive boons, being so vastly outnumbered was still a sore disadvantage, and the captain ground his teeth while staring at the ground for inspiration…

THUD. Another heavy blow was dealt to the large doors, shaking the entire room.

"We could always surrender." One of the soldiers said timidly.

"We don't surrender." Hark replied, his voice aflame. "Or would you rather have lawless mercenaries raiding your homeland before the year's end, ravaging away everything you love!"

The soldier stepped back, surprised by such sudden passion. Not a moment later though, a universal gasp went out as Torric struck the noble across the jaw with his fist.

"Don't talk like you know what it's like to lose something." The young man spat.

"Soldier! You are out of line!" The captain shouted, his hand on the hilt of his sword. "That is your lord you are speaking to!"

"No." Hark interrupted, raising his hand in forbearance. "It's fine. He has made his point."

The captain started back for the third time in those few minutes, and then nodded his head. "Very well, sir."

THUD. Another heavy impact on the doors.

"Alright! We hold the castle or die trying." The captain ordered at last. "The heir is right: we have to draw the line here – in our own blood if need be. We might not live to see the morning, but by the gods we'll be men."

The small band of soldiers steeled their countenances and nodded in acceptance as they turned to face their leader. Behind them, crackling could be heard as the door was lit ablaze – time was running short.

"The hallway on the bottom floor and the halls at the top of each set of stairs are thin enough one man can hold it." The captain said. "We split into three detachments: one holds the center hall, and one holds each of the upper hallways. Hur, you stay to the middle hall, it will be the most heavily attacked most likely – do your best to help the soldiers there. If any of you see the man in front of you fall, I want you to take his place and fight twice as hard. Remember that if any of these three halls are taken, the castle belongs to our enemies. Is that understood?"

"Yes sir!" Torric and his comrades answered in unison, saluting.

"Good. Now split up." The captain concluded.

Torric obeyed the command and headed for one of the staircases, planning on following the few men he recognized. It was then that he felt a hand on his shoulder and turned around; Hark was standing before him.

"I have no business with you, high-born." The young man said.

"I know." Was the humble but unafraid reply. "But I saw you have no shield."

Torric looked down to see the iron kite that had been fastened to Hark's forearm being offered to him.

"It would be of more use in the hands of a live soldier than the grasp of a dead noble."

The shield was dropped into Torric's hand before he could respond, and by the time he looked up, Hark had already joined the defense in the middle hall. Amazed by such generosity, the young soldier looked toward the noble for a moment… and then snorted and headed to his post, strapping the iron kite to his arm.

The door was fully ablaze by that time, and with each blow of the battering ram chunks of burning wood were sprayed across the stone floor. Nevertheless, Torric reached his position as the second to last man in the hallway at the top of the righthand stairs; three other soldiers ahead of him and one behind.

THUD… THUD… THUD. The battering ram beat. A countdown to a hopeless battle. THUD… THUD… CRASH! The door shattered at last and Kasil regulars began pouring in like termites! Torric could not see the door from where he stood, but he could hear the shouts of charging warriors, and made ready – shield up, sword at his side, grip strong, feet apart, knees bent, eyes sharp. Three men ahead of him. If they fell, it was his duty to fight on with greater strength. If he fell, that duty belonged to the man behind him. And if that man too was slain… their allies would be lost, along with the castle.

The thought occurred to him that if any of the other groups failed the penalty would be the same. That was how little it would take for all of them to be defeated; one detachment of five men falling short or giving up. Torric ground his teeth together in defiance of such grim thoughts, and held his sword tighter as his vision began to cloud over with a red fog.

The ally soldier at the front of his row had begun fighting, and around his companions he could see the tide of Kasil invaders he would soon be facing – from the man in the front all of the way down the stairs, and unknown numbers more waiting. Scouts had reported over a hundred Kasil soldiers and mercenaries in the area over the last few days. For such an important assault, doubtless they had brought all of them, not to mention whatever more they might have had that Oser had not learned of.

The soldier at the front of Torric's row fell, and the second one followed close behind. There was now only one man between Torric and the endless waves of foes. If – no – *when* he died, it would be his turn to fight. Red. Red. Red. Blood. Scales. Fire.

The soldier in front of Torric screamed in pain and dropped to one knee, his leg slashed. Clang. Clang. He deflected two attacks and struck down one more invader, but then his life was taken in retribution. It was Torric's turn at last.

With a cry, the young warrior rushed a few steps forward to meet his enemy and attacked with mad strength. Blood covered his blade as his first foe fell, surprised by the sudden onslaught. Blood is red. Red. Blood. Scales. Fire.

A snowy field appeared, houses ablaze and a dragon roaring. Torric reached out his hand once more, trying to grasp even just the fingertips of his parents. He was a soldier. He was not like the others though. He did not fight for the people he might lose – he had already lost them. Nor did he fight to honor their name. His parents never asked him to be a soldier, neither did that orphan girl he grew up with.

No. He fought because of that color. Red. He fought because of that liquid. Blood. He fought because of that memory. Scales. He fought because of that pain. Fire. An inescapable memory, an undying misery, carved into his heart and driving his every action. He fought not for honor or selflessness or fame or greed or pride. He fought because the only hope he had was in those three departed lives. Mother. Father. Sister. And the only reason he had to live was to see their faces again.

Red. Blood. Scales. Fire.

The siege of Castle Walsin eventually ended in defeat for the forces of Oser. Torric was wounded and surrendered when Kasil soldiers attacked from both sides and struck down the man behind him. Those odds alone, of course, were not enough to undo his rage and battle frenzy, but the invaders proceeded to back away and inform him that his remaining allies had already laid down their arms, and his captain himself had ordered the surrender.

Torric was enraged, but dropped his weapon and submitted, if for no other reason than to later strike the coward of a captain – should he ever be given an opportunity. Thus ends, sadly, the tale of the Siege of Castle Walsin. What happened next is another story for another time… one I hope to tell someday soon, I might add.

…

William woke up to the sound of the rooster's crow and got out of bed, careful not to disturb his sleeping wife. She was often up as early or even earlier than he, and therefore her continued slumber was something precious that he dared not harm. Therefore, bending over, the farmer kissed his bride on the cheek before heading out of the house; after all, the sun would not wait for him.

Once outside, the first place he went was the blacksmith's shop: the workbench was empty and the fire out, but the coals were still hot. Turning around, William returned to his home and checked the back room: it too was empty.

Leaving through the backdoor, the villager headed out into the field. After a few minutes of walking, he could hear the sound he had been listening for; a rhythmic cutting of the air, accompanied by the chiming sound of metal on metal. A few more moments passed and he could see the man he was seeking: Torric, the Knight of Heaven; clad in iron, with a gleaming sword in his hand and a flawless shield on his arm.

The knight swung and thrust, parried invisible blows, and raised his shield in defense against unseen ghosts. His daily training. His daily discipline.

He was a soldier. He was not like the others though. He did not fight for the people he might lose – he had already lost them. Nor did he fight to honor their name. His parents never asked him to be a soldier, neither did that orphan girl he grew up with.

He fought not for honor or selflessness or fame or greed or pride.

He did not fight for himself or any mortal being.

He was a soldier. Yes. He was a knight. The best. And he fought for the Being above all others. He fought for the God of love and truth and hope.

He, Torric, Knight of Heaven, fought… for the All-King.

Appendix A
(Names and Pronunciation)

Amboros	am – boar – oh – ss
Blackhound	black – hound
Chila	chee – luh
Chobo	cho – bow
Furbos	fur – bow – ss
Garnage	gar – neh – dge
Jadu	jaw – dew
Kasil	caw – sill
Hanny	haw – knee
Lilula	lie – lew – luh

Lilu	lie – lew
Lula	lew – luh
Lala	law – law
Oser	oh – sir
Torric	tore – rick
Valtara	v – all – tar – uh
Walsin	wall – sin
Wyvern	why – vern

Appendix B
(The Primary Races of Alataran)

The world of Alataran (all – ah – tar – an) is home to many different races of demi-humans, as well as humans themselves. All of these races share a few common traits, namely, they are roughly human in form and function, and they possess sentience. Over the centuries many of the original races have gone extinct or thinned so much as to be thought so, and new ones have emerged. At the time of this story, there are fifteen "Primary" races. These Primary races are the ones still commonly known to exist, and with notable numbers remaining.

These are:

Humans

The first and oldest of the Alataran races, and honored for this position by all others being named *demi*-human. Although physically inferior to most other races in some way, humans somehow still hold a place amongst the fifteen Primary races. Pushed to the brink of extinction time and time again, they have declared by their tenacity, more than once, that they will not go quietly into the night, but instead will remain so long as the world does.

Cheribimi (chair – i – bih – mee)

A race angelic in appearance, Cheribimi are bright and varied in their looks but always share the same celestial air. Although not angels or spirits, they possess similar powers – wings, healing, and natural serenity. Their native land of the White Spire prizes unity and creativity.

Diabli   (die   –   ob   –   lee)

A race demonic in appearance, coming in all sizes, shapes, and colors, but still always giving off a sinister air. Although not actual demons or spiritual beings, the Diabli's powers are similar. Stronger, faster, and tougher than humans, they also possess a broader appetite that includes raw organs. Wings, claws, night vision, and fire are all tools at their disposal. Their native land of the Black Spire encourages individuality and freedom.

Draco   (dray   –   co)

Dragon-like and powerful, the Draco are named after the reptilian titans of legend. With scales like iron, and fiery breath, they are rightly considered one of the most dangerous of all the races. Throughout their history two main breeds, the Eastern Draco with their wings, and the Western Draco with their harder scales, have battled for dominance. Nowadays they have an uneasy peace on their united homeland, Dragar (drag- are).

Ursa   (er   –   suh)

As large and strong as the bears they resemble, the Ursa are powerful demi-humans that combine the stature of a man with the strength of a bear. Their name comes from the bear constellations of the sky, and is an ode to the natural connection most Ursa feel with the stars. Their homeland of Orus (or – us) offers brilliant canopies of the night sky, and harbors peace whenever possible.

Gremlin   (grem   –   lin)

Mad and shortsighted, many question if they are indeed sentient and should even be counted amongst the demi-human races. Gremlins are twisted in appearance, with lanky limbs and large heads that are necessary to support their massive jaws and teeth. Despite this apparent malformation they are incredibly strong and agile, although equally weak-minded. The wasteland they call home is named Groa (grow – uh), a desert inhospitable to most any other race.

Naga   (na   –   guh)

Resembling large snakes with arms and legs, the Naga are popularly considered untrustworthy and treacherous. Their homeland of Shanzar (shan – zar) does not at all abate this reputation of them. Embroiled for decades in feudal wars of schemes, murders, and heinous crimes committed by all factions, the island is mostly left alone by the other nations – although brave traders do still come to its shores for commerce from time to time.

Ninelives   (nine   –   lives)

Catlike demi-humans with fantastic dexterity and grace. As curious as the animals they resemble, these adventurous spirits are naturally at home on the continent of Malpaka (mall – pock – uh) – a large country of many unmapped savannahs and jungles – all of which they have claimed as their own. Ninelives are generally considered undependable, but a sort of natural charisma about them largely charms away this opinion and keeps them respected.

Pak   (pack)

Doglike demi-humans resembling the popular werewolves of human lore. Their exceptional sense of smell makes them natural trackers, and their keen night vision expands this skill into deadly hunting. It is well known that Pak are social beings, finding their greatest strength and purpose in living alongside one another. Their homeland, Tarfa (tar – fuh), is a long island with arid deserts to the south, rugged mountains to the north, and woodland between.

Razaan   (ray   –   zan)

A warrior race of aquatic demi-humans with the gills, fins, and teeth of sharks. Razaan are ferocious hunters and fighters with incredible prowess both above and below the water's surface. Their homeland, Ar-Uk (are – ook), is dominated by a strength-worshipping culture where those with exceptional physical might are honored and the physically inferior are generally treated poorly.

Shrime   (shrime)

Sometimes known as "mushroom-men", Shrime resemble a strange mix between a human and the common fungus. While lacking in physical strength, Shrime possess impressive agility and a large variety of unique traits – everything from how they eat and breathe, to their ability to quickly fabricate tools and apparel of exceptional design and craftsmanship. Their homeland, Mon, is a dense swamp that most other races struggle to navigate. The Shrime themselves are generally peaceful and trustworthy, bound by a strong sense of honor.

Skorma-Hive (score – muh)

By far the strangest of all recorded demi-human races, Skorma Hives – or just Skorma, as they are typically called – are each an animated nest in the shape of a humanoid body, inhabited by a hive of sentient insects. The matriarch Queen of each nest functions as the mind of the body, and shares its sentience with each and every one of its subordinate workers and soldiers, while also leaving them to their various tasks within the body as a whole. Scholars often remark that the Skorma are a living embodiment of unity. The Skorma homeland, simply called, Collective, is a socialist nest island governed primarily by female officers of various duties, dedicated to the preservation of itself.

Velveteen (velvet – een)

Rabbit-like demi-humans, the Velveteen are often misjudged as week or cowardly due to their soft fur and "cute" appearance. For the natives of the Velveteen homeland, Gash, this is true only of the women, children, and few men who have not chosen to fight. Rival warlords and their warbands regularly clash across the prairies and forests of the island, striking fear into the hearts of any who do not take up arms, and instilling an attitude of fearful submission until they will no longer oppose any atrocity or injustice.

Xilvian (zil – vie – an)

Considered majestic by some, beautiful by others, and horrific by the rest, Xilvian are indeed a strange looking race of demi-human. A third eye decorates their forehead, antlers like those of a deer sprout from their crowns, insect wings like a dragonfly's unfold from their backs, hooves clatter on the ground beneath them instead of feet, and gills adorn their necks, giving them an otherworldly air. The Xilvian homeland, a chain of tropical islands called Yien (yee – en), is a commercial giant and military superpower possessing some of the most advanced technological inventions to have ever graced the surface of Alataran.

Zrell (zrehl)

Savage, vicious hunters from a cursed land of darkness and desecration. These scaled giants have razor sharp claws capable of shredding through even strong metals and enormous jaws known to devour entire portions of their enemies whole. Their home island, Galtora (gall – tor – uh), is a wasteland of rocks and eternal storms. Beneath its surface, however, is where the Zrell live – wandering vast cave networks in hopes of finding stray food or water; fighting, killing, and struggling simply to survive.

Acknowledgements

My thanks go first and greatest to the Almighty God who supplied me with creativity, freedom, time, skill, and energy to write this – not to mention his countless blessings beside.

Next I thank my family and friends for supporting me.

My proofreaders deserve applause for their aid and diligence in helping me make this work into a reality. As well as the artist responsible for the cover.

And last but not least, I thank you, the reader, for taking time out of your life to immerse yourself in this product of my mind. I hope it found you well and offered encouragement and relief in the midst of the storms of this world.

Until next time, God bless you, one and all,

- R.J. Knight

HERO'S TALE

BLOOD

THUNDER

R.J. Knight

Other Books by R.J. Knight

Hero's Tale THE SERPENT'S HEIR

Jadu's story continues as his destiny is made manifest – to destroy all that he loves. Prophesy has spoken and only one of the Serpent's Heirs can save Tarfal, but a beast lurks in this hero's heart, and in every future where he is seen nothing but death follows.

GRIMOIRE

Can six college students put aside their differences and overcome an ancient and powerful evil before it is too late? Will they even survive?

PROPHET

The sequel to *Grimoire*, this is an action-packed story full of suspense, courage, faith, and love, every bit as intriguing as its predecessor.

Hero's Tale RISE OF COURAGE

The origin story of a young Razaan whose dreams of adventure become nightmares when he is forced onto a lifelong quest for glory and honor that he never wanted.

Hero's Tale PATH OF THE GLORY-SEEKER

Raalumus's story continues as he seeks out glory and honor for his people. But as his adventures become ever more and more perilous, he is faced with a question – at what cost? Is any price to great to offer on the altar of glory?

CHROMA DIARIES, free on Wattpad

The first-person narrative of a disembodied mechanical head who watches as a misfit band of two royals, an accountant, an intern, and a pilot with a few too many split personalities make new allies and try to save the world.

www.ingramcontent.com/pod-product-compliance
Lightning Source LLC
Chambersburg PA
CBHW070339130626
46556CB00007B/2938